Content Warnings: Abuse (Physical, Emotional), Violence, Fantasy Violence

Cover and Frontispiece created by: Joshua Stolte & Antony Soehner

antonysoehner.com

To Nick and Andy, it's not "Tres Reyes" without either of you. Be careful and don't get lost!

ACKNOWLEDGMENTS

To my friends and family for their never-ending love and support.
To my amazing friend, Josh, without whom these stories would never come to life.
To my amazing editor, Cate, who turns my ramblings into immaculate stories with me.
And to you, reader. Thank you for supporting and coming along for the adventures. This isn't possible without you.

THE PRINCE

BY ANTONY SOEHNER

Contents

I. A Prince is Born

II. Kingdom in Black

III. King's Philosophy

IV. The Princess

V. Friends and Family

VI. Mother's Nightmare

VII. Alice and Olsdeyr

VIII. Ashti the Brave

IX. The Tankard Knight

X. Improvising Destiny

XI. The Wailing Forest

XII. Waking Up

XIII. Ta'goda

XIV. Ancestor's Dance

XV. Feast of the Harvest

XVI. Medicine Witches

XVII. Man in the Mask

XVIII. Escape to the Riverlands

XIX. River Wolf

XX. Under the Moon

XXI. Burning Eagle

XXII. Campfire Coffee

XXIII. Riding the Plains

XXIV. The Lost Knight

A PRINCE IS BORN

The king paced outside of his own bedchamber. He focused on the click of his boots against the stone floor in hopes it would drown the howls of pain coming from the other side of the massive, solid oak door.

The castle was otherwise silent as the queen's screams echoed through the empty halls, making the king uneasy. The last two times they did this he was met by swarms of people excitedly congratulating him on the birth of his new heir.

Through the window carved into the stone wall, the king watched the midnight rainstorm continue to batter down hard against the castle walls. He walked over to the window and glanced out upon his kingdom.

Out of this particular window, the king could see the entire eastern side of the town outside his castle's walls. The streets were abandoned as people took shelter from the heavy rain. He watched a cloaked figure in the distance ushering mud-covered people into the dimly lit horse stables.

CRACK!

Lightning struck the fields outside the town.

The king stared out toward the dark horizon, watching the smoke quickly vanish as it was attacked by falling rain.

CRACK!

The lightning was getting closer, striking the middle of a road and hitting a wagon on the edge of town.

His eyes followed the dark road towards the castle's outer gates but stopped just before the walls.

Outside the eastern wall was a familiar square within the kingdom, built around a single statue and made to accommodate thousands of people in front of the king's castle. Fairs and festivals were staged in the open courtyard. Coronation ceremonies used to be celebrated there, and funerals were mourned in the massive plaza.

The king felt something tug on his heart as he stared down at the golden mighty statue in the middle of the square.

"Watch all you'd like, wretched old man," the king snarled under his breath, "this is my kingdom now. Your legacy is obsolete. Soon, you will be nothing but a forgotten king." He spat out the window towards the statue. "May you burn in hell."

CRACK!

The king jumped back from the window as a bolt of lightning exploded against the top of the statue. The thunder rolled and the king composed himself. He peered back out the window and saw the decapitated head of the statue laying on the cobblestone.

He glared down into the lifeless eyes of his grandfather's golden face. "A sign from the divine," the king whispered to himself with vanity.

He was abruptly torn from his moment of triumph as he heard his queen's scream fill the castle again from inside his chambers followed by the cries of a newborn child. The sound of a new life.

The king turned back out the window one last time to scorn his grandfather's legacy, but when he looked down to where the statue's head landed, it was gone. Slowly, he scanned his eyes up and found the head back on top of the statue where it had always been.

The king rubbed his eyes in disbelief.

"Your Majesty," a sheepish nurse appeared in the slightly opened doors to his bedchamber, "the queen has requested your presence."

The king lingered at the window for a moment, trying to understand what he'd just witnessed. Then he turned towards the nurse with a nod before following her into his chambers.

The fireplace crackled under the infant's screams. The king approached the huddle of women dressed in white who crowded around the large bed.

When he stopped at the foot of the bed, the women dispersed with their heads bowed, revealing an exhausted queen holding the small bundle in her arms tightly against her chest.

She lay in the massive bed with nothing but a blanket from her waist down. Her long, thick mane of curly, brunette hair was disheveled, and a mess compared to the usual tight braid she would wear beneath her crown. Her cheeks were rosy while the rest of her face was pale and covered in beads of sweat.

She smiled down into the bundle in her arms and whispered happily into it. She looked up and her eyes locked with the king's. Her joyful expression vanished as she held the bundle tighter to her chest.

The king raised his chin and glared down at her, stirring the uncomfortable tension in the room.

"Leave us," the king commanded.

The nurses and midwives bowed their heads before swiftly exiting the chamber.

"Not you," the king clipped.

The shortest member of the flock of nurses froze just before the door as the rest flooded into the empty hall and closed the doors.

"A Princess does not hide with the help," the king said without breaking eye contact with the queen.

"Yes, Your Majesty," the young girl bowed her head.

"This is the last time I want to see you around those people. You are royalty and you will act like it," the king demanded calmly.

"Yes, Your Majesty," the princess bowed her head.

"Now, come and be a part of my family," the king commanded. He extended his arm towards the princess and motioned for her to come closer.

The young girl turned around and removed the nurse's bonnet on her head in reluctant defeat, releasing a long, coiled braid that dropped down her back. The young face of the princess stared back at the king before hesitantly approaching his hand.

Without a warning, the king grabbed her by the wrist and wrapped his arm around her shoulders.

She tried to fight back but he tightened his grip around her so she couldn't move.

"Now that we're all here as a family," the king grunted, swinging his daughter around so the two of them could see the queen.

"Alice," the queen spoke to the princess, calmly masking her own emotions, and remaining stoic before her daughter, "I want you to meet your brother, Theodore."

"Theodore?" the king frowned, "that isn't the name I decided on."

"I know," the queen sighed as she darted her eyes back to the king in disdain, "when he's old enough to decide whether he wants to wear your crown, he can decide if he wants to share your name."

"Enough of this," the king snapped at his queen, causing the newborn baby to erupt into another fit of crying. He dropped his tight grip around Alice's shoulders and stood at the bedside. "Give me my child!" he demanded as he began forcing the baby from the queen's arms.

"No, George, no! What are you going to do with my baby? George, please don't hurt him. Not another one of our—" the queen begged hysterically.

The king ripped the child from her with one hand and slapped her across the face with the other. "I am the king of this castle and the head of this family! My demands will be respected and my authority will be recognized! If this is to be the heir to my crown then he will take the name of the king who blessed him with his life."

Alice rushed to her mother's side and held her as she cried helplessly on her shoulder. The princess glared back at the king with a hateful fury.

He returned the look with an icy stare. "You will know your place as well. Come and welcome your next king."

"No," the princess growled.

"I will not be disobeyed by my own daughter. There will be no second warning. Stand by your king and welcome his heir or I will—" the king froze as his eyes met the fire within the queen's scorn. In a moment of panic, the king turned with the baby in his arms and stormed out of the chamber.

"George, no!" the queen cried from her bed.

"Disrespected in my own castle—in my own chamber!" the king hissed under his breath. "They don't understand what I've sacrificed for them. No one will ever understand. But I will show them all. Everything in this world will be ours!" The king marched through the long corridor with the child now screaming in his arms. He pushed through the satin drapes that prevented the outside world from seeing inside his grand hall.

He stood on the balcony that overlooked the eastern square with the statue of his grandfather.

"Look unto me, foul old man, look unto me and weep with anger!" the king shouted into the stormy night sky. The rain continued to pour from above, drenching the king and his newborn child. He raised the bundled child above his crown towards the stormy sky. "You were a fool to try and deny me my birthright! I hope that while you're burning in hell, you can see what I have become. I will conquer this world and this will be my heir to see its glory. He will one day rule and his subjects will know of my eternal power. You will be forgotten in the history that I will write!"

The wind began to kick up and rain came down harder. The streets flooded and lightning cracked across the dark horizon one after the other.

"That's right you weak, old bastard!" the king screamed into the sky. "Try to smite me now! You're obsolete—forgotten, just like you said I would become! I'm the most powerful being in this world and I hold the key to my people's everlasting worship! I am the Eternal King! I will burn it all down and erect my throne from the ashes I leave behind!"

CRACK!

A bolt of lightning struck the head of the golden statue again.

As the king slowly looked down to the plaza to see the damage, the entire statue was destroyed. There was nothing left but the small stone plinth that the statue once stood on.

The king smiled as he stared down at the site where his grandfather's memorial had vanished.

"My loyal subjects!" the king cried out into the flooding city. "Come out to the streets and greet your new Prince! The heir to my throne, your future king! Long live the king, long live King George the Second!"

CRACK!

KINGDOM IN BLACK

The streets were filled with people dressed in black and an eerie silence laid across the kingdom beneath the castle. The occasional sniffle or whimper would echo through the somber streets. Not even a screaming child would break the heaviness that loomed over the world.

Church bells began to ring through the kingdom. The crowds turned their heads towards the castle and as a collective, the people cleared the streets, making a path from the front gates.

A steady beat of drums filled the streets, playing into the off beats of the church bells. As the ringing faded, the drums continued to the sounds of marching.

Two massive golden gates with twisting designs slowly opened inward, and a procession of guards began marching together out of the castle walls.

Hundreds of dignified soldiers with their swords in scabbards and their arms swinging at their sides marched in tandem. Each step was a thunderous clap against the cobblestone. Between every dozen rows was a line of cavalry soldiers on horseback holding longbows in one hand and the reins in the other.

The parade of soldiers went on for a long while and was followed by more marching. Armored Knights, some on horseback, others marching on foot holding the banners of the king and the kingdom's flag. Surrounded by the knights was an ornate horse-drawn wagon.

On the back of the open cart was a casket draped in a curtain of black lace. A wreath of pink and white flowers rested on the lid.

The casket wheeled through the town where people deep in mourning tossed white roses into the street. Some people handed handfuls of flowers to the knights who would accept them and place them on the wagon around the casket.

Behind the wagon were more knights who surrounded three people shrouded in black garments. In the middle walked the king. His head was held high and his jaw, tightly stoic beneath his beard. He wore his grand, double-breasted, high collared black coat and the royal sashes underneath. Secured beneath the golden epaulets of his coat's right shoulder were three golden braided aiguillettes and his left shoulder was cloaked in a black, half-cape that draped to his knee. Atop his brow was the seven-point, golden crown with a single black gem in the center.

The sun glinted off the crown as the king stepped out from behind the castle gates. Seconds later, the sky started to grow dark as massive gray clouds rolled in over the kingdom.

Behind the king and to his left marched a young woman. Princess Alice. She wore a long, black dress that brushed the ground and masked her steps. Her silver tiara rested on top of her forehead and acted as the anchor for the black veil that masked her face. In front of her chest on display, she held another crown similar to the king's but smaller and cast in silver.

Directly to her right was a young man dressed similarly to

the king. The mop of long, curly, black hair was matted down over his brow by the five-point, golden crown with a single black gem on his head, making it hard to fully see. He was a slender young man but he came eye to eye with the princess.

Bouncing at his hip was a silver saber in its sheath. Unlike the king and princess, he kept his head down trying to avoid eye contact with the people watching them walk.

The young boy was Prince George, Heir to the throne—or as he preferred to be known—Theo.

The procession went on for another couple of miles behind them. Dignitaries of the king, his dukes, duchesses, generals, allies, governors, and so on.

Slowly, they made their way through the town and the long march brought them to the church that faced the castle from across the town.

The ranks of soldiers and knights broke off from the casket and began clearing the church's perimeter fence of bystanders and people trying to watch.

Coming to a halt at the front steps of the church, the wagon waited for the king and his children.

Once the important people were inside the church gates, a handful of knights who didn't break off proceeded to surround the wagon. With a single command, eight knights hoisted the casket onto their shoulders, letting the ends of the black lace drape their arms, and they marched into the church.

The wagon was relocated and the king, princess, and Theo walked up the stairs. They stopped at the massive entryway to the church and then turned to face the others behind them. One by one the dignitaries gave their condolences to the royal family as they entered the chapel.

There was no sign of cracking on the king's face. He didn't show any sadness or pain. He kept his stoic composure as he thanked each individual for their condolences.

Alice was visibly distraught, but she was holding it together. There was sorrow, anger, and pain burning in her heart, but her words came out calm and sophisticated.

Theo continued to avoid eye contact. He'd never been in this situation before and all he felt was uncomfortable. He didn't know what to do and he didn't like being on display like this.

"Prince George," the king grunted under his breath as there was a small break in the line of guests. "Pick your head up and greet your people. Show them you are strong."

Theo gritted his teeth, his jaw tightening with anger. "Yes, Your Majesty," he clipped.

As he looked up, he met an old woman's eyes staring back at him. She was wrinkled and had curled gray hair hidden behind a black veil. She barely came to Theo's chest but her presence made her seem like she was a giant.

"Prince Theo," she greeted him. She had a smile fixed on her face but he could feel the somberness in her tone. "My condolences to you and your family. Your mother was very dear to me—"

"Thank you," Theo cut her off.

Her smile slipped for a moment but then returned and she nodded. Without another word, the woman shuffled her way into the church.

They continued to greet each guest for the next twenty minutes and when the final guest entered the church, the bells began to ring one last time. Theo and Alice turned into the church, followed by the king, and they took their places in the front pew.

When the bells fell silent again and the drumming finally ceased, the massive wooden doors of the church were swung shut.

Inside, the packed chapel was silent. The casket was placed on the altar and flowers were scattered on the floor beneath.

A man came through a side door at the front of the church wearing white robes and a large hat atop his head. In his hands, he carried a tall, golden staff that stood taller than he did, and a black leather book tucked in his arm. Behind him were two young boys dressed in ceremonial black robes. They both carried incense lanterns filled with burning herbs and their scents filled the chamber. The three approached the altar and stood quietly behind the casket.

The man in white stepped closer to the casket, cleared his throat, and he tapped the staff against the marble floor three times. It echoed into the high church ceiling.

"Your Majesty," the man spoke, acknowledging the king in the front row. "Lords and ladies, dukes and duchesses, our fellow friends and other distinguished guests of His Majesty. We are gathered here today in mourning. For our king's great empire aches at the passing of its noble queen."

He stopped and turned to one of the boys to his left. The boy produced a small chain of wooden beads from his robes and handed it to the man. He turned and carefully placed the chain in a ritual manner atop the casket.

"In her life," the man continued, "she served our kingdom and our king valiantly. She was a faithful wife to His Majesty and a loving mother to his three children."

Theo's ears perked up. He glanced over to the king and his sister who didn't budge at the priest's words.

Maybe he misspoke. Theo thought in his head.

"Her duty to our people was one unparalleled by her predecessors. A humble commoner brought into the castle by the love she shared with our glorious king."

This is starting to turn into praise for my father rather than mourning for my mother, Theo thought.

"She brought humble roots and prosperity to our empire. Her marriage to His Majesty brought full bellies to our people, homes to our homeless, and courage to our brave soldiers. She was the people's queen." The priest paused again.

The entire room turned and looked back towards the entrance of the church as another young boy slowly marched down the aisle with a large bowl of water.

When the boy reached the altar, the priest walked around, and with a quick splash of his hands, he began flicking the water over the casket.

"We call out to the lord of our divine king," the priest said towards the ceiling, "we pray to you and ask that you guide his queen into your care to share eternity in glory. We beg you to look upon her and absolve her of sin so that she may shepherd us when we cross over into your care." He continued splashing the water onto the casket.

Theo was still distracted by the 'three children' comment.

Maybe I just didn't hear him. I haven't been paying attention. He thought to himself.

"May you take her to see her mother and father. May she be blessed by the presence of the king-father and king-mother," the priest proclaimed to the ceiling as he returned to his original spot behind the casket. "And may she once again hold her late son tightly to her chest."

Theo grew anxious. What was this man talking about? Did he really have a dead brother that nobody told him existed? His mind started to spiral as it tried to piece together the priest's words with what he knew.

Nothing connected.

"May we lay our beloved queen to rest," the priest said, pulling Theo back into reality. "As per her wishes, she will be laid in state for her people to mourn before being entombed into the royal mausoleum for her final rest."

It's over? Theo thought as his shoulders sank.

She was finally gone for good. He couldn't believe it.

The king was the first to rise from his seat. Every guest in the church reacted by sliding out of their seats and kneeling before him.

He walked up to the casket as if he were calculating in his head with every step. The priest and the three young boys all bowed their heads and stepped back from the casket.

There was something about how he stood there. Staring at the black lace veil that draped over his queen. He placed a hand on the fabric, clutching his fist, and then releasing it as his jaw went tight.

"Get her out of here," the king grunted under his breath.

His rough and quiet words echoed softly through the church.

"But, Your Majesty—" the priest squeaked.

"Take her to the mausoleum," the king intensified, his fist clenched around the pommel of his sword.

The priest stood there frozen.

"Take her there, now!" The king burst out, slamming his fist on the casket lid as his voice boomed through the church.

"Y—yes, Your Majesty," the priest stuttered, bowing his head.

In haste, the eight knight pallbearers surrounded the casket, lifted it over their shoulders again, and marched away with the queen.

The king spun around on his heels, his cape billowing behind him, and he stormed out of the church.

Alice grabbed Theo's arm aggressively and ushered him after the king.

"Alice, stop, you're hurting me," Theo begged. "Let me go. I want to say goodbye to her—"

"Shut up!" Alice hissed through her teeth. "Just do as I say. Trust me."

"Alice," Theo whined.

"I said shut up and do what I say."

Theo sighed and followed his sister. They hurried after the king who was now angrily walking back the way they came.

Knights and guardsmen began chaotically pushing commoners back from the king's path, unprepared for the sudden outburst.

Theo watched as people were screaming and crying as the guards forced them back violently. At one point he saw a knight in full armor strike an elderly man in the head with their shield. The old man fell backward into the crowd, lost in a sea of legs.

He turned to stop the knight who was now forcing a woman clutching a baby to the ground. But Alice quickly snatched his arm again and pulled him behind her.

"What are you—" Theo snapped at her.

"I told you to do two things. Shut up and listen to me," Alice grit through her teeth again. "It's for your own—for *our* own good."

But Theo couldn't take his eyes off the scene.

The knight rolled the struggling woman over and began grabbing the baby in her arms. She fought back but the knight was too strong. He ripped the bundled child from the mother and two other guards lifted the woman by her arms to carry her away.

"Let her go!" Theo shouted, cutting through the screams of chaos.

The entire city fell silent once again and everything froze as all eyes turned on Theo.

He broke free from his sister's grasp and raced over to the knight who took the baby. Without argument, the knight turned the child over to the young prince and knelt at his feet.

As he cradled the baby in the fold of his elbow, the sky went gray, and with a flash, rain fell from the clouds.

The baby started to scream and cry as the drops fell on its face.

Theo carried the baby back to its mother who was weeping on her knees in the muddy street.

She trembled before Theo as he knelt down and offered her child back. Without warning, she sprang forward and wrapped her arms around Theo and the baby in a hug.

The three knights lurched forward drawing their swords.

"Cease!" a booming voice bellowed from outside the scene in the street. It was the king's voice.

Theo turned his head and the woman released him as she took her baby.

The king's face wasn't angry. Even his body remained stoic in posture. But Theo could see the fire in his eyes.

"Release her and the child," the king demanded.

The three knights put their swords back on their hips and stood at attention facing the king. The woman rose to her feet with her child pressed to her chest. She turned to the king with a deep bow.

"Thank you, Your Majesty. Bless you. Long may you reign," the woman stuttered out nervously. She turned in embarrassment and vanished into the soaked crowd.

"You three," the king bellowed at the three knights, "escort the prince back into the castle."

KING'S PHILOSOPHY

Theo hadn't taken more than two steps into the castle's courtyard when the king halted in front of him.

"Leave us," the king commanded.

The three knights walked backward down the stairs, leaving Theo alone with the king.

"This will be my only warning," the king clipped without turning to face Theo, "you will refrain from making a fool of your king in front of his people."

"Father—"

King George whipped his arm around. With the back of his heavily ringed hand, he struck Theo across the side of his head and face. One of the rings snagged the bridge of his nose, leaving a deep gash in the middle of his face.

Theo could feel the warm liquid pooling in his hands as he held his face and collapsed to his knees in a daze of white pain.

"I am your king!" he snarled through the ringing in Theo's ears. "Your purpose is to obey me as your king and know your place beneath me. You think that because you are the heir to *my* throne, I would allow you to disrespect me without consequence? Those people are beneath us both and any of them could try to take that from me. That woman could have been an assassin or one of those disgusting animals on the eastern border. She could have killed me!"

"She was holding a child," Theo groaned through the manic daze. He tried to stop the blood flowing from the gaping slash across his face but it kept pouring through his fingers.

"But it was a risk and could have ended my life! My empire was at stake!" The king shouted.

For a moment, the king looked down upon his wounded son in disgust. He slowly raised his hand to the hilt of his sword and with a click, the blade came free of its scabbard. But something caught his eye and he froze. Light glinted off the white silver saber hooked to Theo's belt. The Queen's Saber.

The king clicked his sword back into its sheath and let it dangle from his waist again.

"I will send someone to come clean you up," the king clipped as he turned on his heels. "I want you to remember that everything I do is for you... don't make me regret it."

Theo swallowed as the threat struck his ears. He was in no shape to fight with the king.

After a while, the rain washed some of the blood from his face. He started to feel chilled and his abdomen was shivering uncontrollably as his blood slowly dripped onto the cobblestones of the courtyard.

It felt like hours before a woman in a faded, tattered pink dress and a stained, white-ish apron came hobbling towards him with a bowl and some rags. She knelt down and tried to help Theo to his feet.

He was still disoriented and struggled to get himself up. When he finally managed to find his legs, the woman slung his arm over her shoulder and tried her best to help the prince into the castle.

This woman was half the size of Theo and nearly three times

his age but she managed to get him safely to the other side of the castle grounds and into his chambers. She carefully laid Theo on the cold stone floor as two more women in similar clothes came into the room with pitchers and rags.

The first woman in the faded pink dress tried to prop Theo up against the foot of his bed. She said something to one of the other women in a language he didn't understand.

Quickly, the other woman began tossing pillows off the bed for the first woman to put behind Theo's back to hold him up.

"What're you—saying?" Theo mumbled out. He was starting to go faint as his sight tunneled to a small point.

He tried to focus on the woman who was washing the wound but the pain was making it harder and harder to stay conscious. Every gentle pat of the cold, wet rags caused Theo to jump or wince.

"Deep breaths, Your Highness," the woman instructed him calmly as she wrung a bloody rag into the bowl.

Another woman leaned over the first woman's shoulder with a cup that she put up to Theo's lips. She carefully tipped the cup and poured the contents into the prince's mouth.

He fought the urge to spit it out but it trickled down his throat before he could stop it. There was a burn as it went down and plummeted like a stone in his stomach. After a couple of seconds, a warm feeling filled him from the inside.

"I apologize, Your Grace," the lady with the cup said as she pulled another cup from a tray behind her and began slowly pouring it into his open wound.

Theo tried to let out a howl of pain as the once encroaching field of black in his vision suddenly shocked white. Then everything went black as Theo passed out from the pain.

The women continued to nurse Theo as he faded in and out of consciousness. The one in the pink dress washed the alcohol from his wound as best she could before the one who grabbed the pillows knelt down in front of the groggy prince.

She wore a faded and muddy yellow dress with a similar, stained apron. She reached into the front pocket of her apron and pulled out a small silver case. It was no bigger than the palm of her hand. She flipped the lid open and revealed a set of silver needles and a spool of fine thread.

Theo regained consciousness for a moment as the woman got closer to his face with the needle. She pressed the sharp point through the layer of skin on one side of his wound. The burning pain caused Theo's eyes to roll back into his head as he passed out again.

The three women worked in tandem as they stitched the prince's face and gently washed his wound.

It was a tedious job stitching the laceration as it went across his face and wasn't all one long scar. It stretched from part of his right cheek and just beneath his eye and across the bridge of his nose. There was a solid gash through the left side of his brow that tapered off just short of the prince's hairline.

After tedious and careful work, the three women relocated the prince and laid him in his bed to apply bandages.

On the bedside table, they left him a bottle of the liquor they had made him drink and a few extra rags.

He never got to thank them nor did he see them again before losing consciousness.

When he finally woke, he was discombobulated and woozy.

"What—happened?" he grunted to himself as the rays of orange sunlight filled his chamber through the open balcony. He raised a hand to his face and winced as he touched the cloth bandages across his nose. "So it wasn't another dream," he assured himself.

He carefully pulled himself from the bed, every muscle in his body ached as if he had just finished a long day sparring with the guards. He noticed that his shirt, jacket, and sashes had been taken off and he was only wearing his pants.

Peering out the window, he caught the final moments of sunlight as the now purple sky faded into the dark blues of night.

"How long—" he murmured to himself.

His head was pounding to the point he could hear it. Without thinking, he reached for the drink left on the table and downed a large swig. He choked as the liquor coated his throat and then splashed in his stomach.

"That's vile," he groaned.

He pulled himself from the bed to his feet and shuffled to the other end. His blood-stained funeral clothes were scattered across the floor and it made him uneasy.

Cupping his hands and submerging them into the basin atop of his vanity, Theo splashed his face with the cold water. It was soothing as the refreshing, cool beads trickled down his cheeks and forehead.

He stared into the foggy mirror set in the wall above the basin. Patches of dried blood still clung to his thick hair. He ran his wet hands through the crusty roots until he was satisfied it was all gone.

Then he noticed something was missing.

"Where's my—" he gasped as he spun around on his heels.

He turned over his entire room searching like a wild beast.

"Where is it?" Theo continued to mutter in panic. Getting more and more annoyed as his searching continued to fail. "Come on. The king is going to—" Theo froze as he suddenly remembered where he lost his crown.

He quickly got to his feet, threw on a robe, and walked out of his chambers into the hallway.

THE PRINCESS

Theo walked across the castle grounds back to the spot his father had berated him. There were little splotches of blood still stained on the stone floors that he used to retrace his steps. After a while of wandering through the halls, he stepped out the front entrance and stood over the now dried pool of blood at the top of the stairs.

He spun around trying to find his crown, hoping it would be sitting at his feet. When he couldn't find it, he turned to give up and go back into the castle. Then a golden glint caught the corner of his eye. It had rolled into a patch of grass next to the grand doorway and was tucked under a small shrub.

He cautiously sauntered over and picked the crown out of the dirt. There was dried mud all over the gem and gold plating.

He placed it on his head and turned to walk back into the castle when he heard faint sounds of a private confrontation coming from within the halls. Not worried about guards catching him wandering the grounds, he started walking back the way he came.

But the conversation grew louder and clearer as he moved through the halls. Theo could hear footsteps echoing down the corridor under the growing voices. It wasn't guards, maids, or servants. He jumped toward the wall and hid behind one of the decorative busts that lined the walls.

"I won't do it!" he heard his sister's voice echo around the corner.

Theo leaned forward a little to see who she was talking to. As she came into view, he saw the king burst out from behind the corner, hastily following Alice.

"That's not an option," the king snarled as he grabbed the princess' arm. He was trying to keep his voice down but his low timbre carried down the hall.

"This is the end of this discussion," Alice clipped, "I won't do it and there is nothing that you can do to make me!"

"I don't recall you having a choice in the matter. As your king, I will be obeyed!" The king demanded. He was beginning to grow angry and his cheeks were turning red beneath his salt and pepper beard.

"As your *daughter*," Alice snapped back, "I won't do it. I would just as soon take my own life than let you manipulate me." She turned in a huff, breaking his grip on her arm, and tried to get away from the king. But before she could take her first step, the king grabbed her by the arm again, tighter than before. Her skin wrinkled and pinched under his angry grasp. "Ow! What are you doing—" Alice cried before the king slapped his other hand over her mouth.

"To secure my bloodline and for the good of my kingdom, you will do as your king commands of you!" the king hissed.

Alice tried to shout for help but nothing more than a muffled scream could be heard through the king's hand.

Theo was petrified as he watched. He had no idea what to do but something deep inside himself screamed at him to intervene. His muscles were frozen, paralyzed in fear. He tried to tell his legs to walk but they wouldn't respond.

"There's no point in screaming, princess," the king's slimy voice plugged Theo's ears.

Anger started to build in his chest. How could he just sit there and ignore what was happening to his sister? The burning emotions swelled in his throat, trying to escape from behind his pursed lips.

"Stop!" Theo shouted from behind the bust. His voice boomed through the castle shaking the entire stone structure around them like an aftershock from an earthquake.

The king stood frozen in the corridor, his hands still tightly gripped over Alice's mouth and around her arm.

Theo's legs carried him out from the shadows and he turned to face the king. The redness of his cheeks had faded for a moment and Theo noticed how pale he looked. But when the king noticed who had caught him, the red returned even brighter.

The king let Alice go and stood up straight, dusting the front of his robes to present himself. He tried to stand tall and moved menacingly towards Theo.

The prince didn't cower. He was numb to whatever was happening and the adrenaline that was coursing through his body was puppeteering him through the moment. That was when his legs carried him towards the king and his sister.

His heart pounded in his chest and between his ears.

He walked past the king, placing himself in front of his sister. Theo felt ten feet tall. Even with the king looming like a tower, the young prince felt like his own glare towered above him.

The king stepped forward into the prince, their noses almost touching. Theo could smell the mead on the king's breath and saw the drunken rage storming in his eyes.

"Now, now, *my son*," the king emphasized, "this is no way to act in front of your princess. You wouldn't harm your *father* in front of her?"

Theo clenched his fists and felt the muscles in his arms tighten. Every fiber in his body was ready to strike the king square in his nose. It burned in the palms of his hands.

Then he felt something wrap around his left arm. In his rage, he turned and looked to see his sister holding his shoulder. She was pulling him back from the king.

All those feelings of anger suddenly washed away. He felt like a massive weight was lifted off his shoulder and he could run forever.

Alice led him through the corridor to the next turn they could take to get out of sight from the king.

Theo watched the king standing like a scarecrow in a field as they fled. He stared with empty, soulless eyes.

The two of them got away, taking the first left Alice could. It was a side hall that went around the grand hall. Alice continued leading until they made it to her bedchamber.

Without invitation, Alice yanked Theo into the room and shut the iron-reinforced, wood doors.

Theo stumbled into the room, catching himself just before falling face-first into one of the dressers. His heart slowed down but the pounding still filled his ears. He could feel the blood racing through his arms and legs. This wave of energy was pulsating and disorienting.

Alice fiddled with the doors, fixed a chair against it, and then rushed over to Theo. She carefully grabbed him by his wrist and elbow.

"You're okay now. Take a deep breath. It's going to be okay," she said calmly as she ushered him towards the bed. She helped him sit down and lay back on the pillows.

Theo tried to regain his breathing but his brain was focused on the anger and desire to fight.

Alice went across the room for a moment and returned with a small, corked vial. She pulled the cork and held it up to Theo's lips. Helping him to sit up, she drained the contents into his mouth.

It had a sweet, citrusy flavor that tingled his tongue while a cool minty sensation coated his throat. He took a deep breath, filling his lungs until he couldn't any longer.

As he exhaled slowly from his nose, he could feel every emotion suddenly escape his body. His mind quieted and he could finally focus on his sister.

"There you go," Alice smiled with relief.

"What was he doing to you?" Theo asked soberly.

"Nothing," Alice clipped, shaking her head. "At least, that's what he says. It isn't anything you should be worried about—"

"He was hurting you," Theo blurted. He pointed at her arm where the king had bruised her in his grasp. "That bastard did hurt you."

Theo wanted to be enraged seeing what his father did to her, but he couldn't feel anything. There was no emotion inside him.

"What was in that vial?" Theo asked. "Why do I feel so... empty?"

Alice sighed and held up the vial. "That was one of my last calming potions."

"You drugged me?" Theo calmly responded. In his head he was furious but he couldn't convey the rage he should be feeling.

"No—kind of— may—okay, yes," Alice deflated.

"Why do you have calming potions?" Theo asked. He was genuinely concerned even though his tone remained dry and lifeless.

"It's something mother taught me," Alice sighed as she spun the empty vial between her thumb and index finger. "I warned you today—in the streets this afternoon. You didn't listen to me and your actions were returned with consequences."

Theo became aware of the scar that would probably remain on his face for the foreseeable future. He was becoming very aware of how exhausted his body suddenly felt. Every muscle ached as he lay there staring at his sister.

"You're lucky, you know?" Alice continued. "Had I done what you did today in front of the entire kingdom, he would have killed me."

"Why do you say that?" Theo tried to frown. He felt his face twitch for a moment but his cheeks didn't move.

"Because he almost did the first time," Alice swallowed. She slipped her left arm out from her gown's shoulder strap.

Theo uncomfortably turned his head away from his sister. "What're you doing?" he grimaced.

"Shut up and look," Alice clipped.

Theo hesitantly looked back at his sister. She pulled her left breast up and away from her left side, exposing a small but noticeable scar at the top of her ribs. It looked as if the dagger was twisted after she was stabbed.

"Who did—" Theo stopped himself, catching a silent look from Alice.

"I was a little younger than you. All because I gave food to people starving outside the gates. He spoke to me with all civility until he got close enough to grab me."

She carefully put her gown back on and brushed her hair back behind her shoulders. "When he twisted the blade, it broke inside the wound and shattered one of my ribs. He told me that if I survived, he would make sure the next punishment wasn't the same."

"What did you do?" Theo perked up. His emotions started to trickle back into his voice.

"The only thing I could do," Alice looked down at the ground, "I told Mom."

"And she stayed here with that monster lurking around?" Theo raised his voice. It was a relief to have his emotions again.

"Keep your voice down!" Alice hissed through her teeth.

"She did it to protect me. To protect all of us. If she had confronted him, he would have killed me, and she couldn't leave him, that would have got her killed."

They both sat uncomfortably in the silence that lingered as they tried to avoid the heart-wrenching topic of their late mother.

"Has he killed before?" Theo asked, trying to ignore the awkwardness.

"The man is a warmonger," Alice clipped, staring at her brother.

"I mean, like family or friends," Theo clarified. "During Mom's funeral, the priest said something about her *three* children. Last time I counted, you and I only made two." He tried to raise his arm to emphasize the two with his fingers, but his muscles felt like sacks of rocks dangling from his shoulders.

Alice averted her eyes from his.

"There was another one!" Theo burst out. "Why didn't I know this? Someone could have told me by now, surely?"

"Theo," Alice said calmly.

"Don't *Theo* me," he exclaimed. He tried to keep his voice down but he was growing furious again.

"Calm down or—"

"Or what? Are you going to force another potion down my throat?" Theo snapped.

"Yes!" Alice cut with an icy glare. "Now shut up and listen!"

FRIENDS AND FAMILY

"You deserve to know," Alice sighed.

Theo painfully sat up in the bed, resting on his elbow.

"We have an older brother. His name is James. He was to become the next king," Alice recalled. "He was a strong leader, an excellent fighter, and an astute politician. There wasn't a being in this world that he couldn't sway. But that posed a threat to the king."

Theo could see the pain in her eyes.

"The two of them clashed and fought constantly as we grew older. The king wanted to spread his empire by conquering his enemies and allies alike. James wanted to unite the world through peaceful diplomacy. Something finally tipped between the two of them one night after James had spoken out against the king and he took it as disrespect. He claimed he was being slandered by his own son in front of his generals. The next morning, he was found dead in his chambers, Mom told me. Rumors spread of suicide throughout the kingdom but I know there was no way. No one ever said what was in the room, only that it was heartbreaking. The story always changed." Alice bit the inside of her lip to stop the quivering and she shifted uncomfortably. "Mom was distraught for a long time after. She hardly spoke or ate. She was a shell of herself. But the king went on like there was nothing wrong. He continued on with his conquests and never again spoke of James."

Alice peered off, staring at the now starry sky outside her balcony. "He sent a thousand men to conquer a fortress atop a steep hill. The conquest took all of two days and by nightfall of the second day, ten men returned from the battle." She returned her eyes to Theo and let out a small sigh.

"How come no one speaks of him?" Theo asked. "Why do I not remember my own brother?"

"The king had him struck from the public eye. Anything attached to his memory was destroyed and removed."

Another silent moment hung over them.

"You really think *he* killed him?" Theo mumbled nervously.

"I don't see who else would have," Alice shrugged.

"That makes me nervous," Theo exhaled as he felt a balloon of anxiety swelling in his chest.

"He gave you a warning already," Alice said, tapping the bridge of her nose.

"And then I defied him again," Theo reminded her. "He's going to kill me, isn't he?"

"He won't," Alice shook her head. "After what happened today, he would be too much of a suspect. You're safe for now. I will make sure of it." Her demeanor quickly shifted from thoughtful to aggressive. "Remember all of this next time I tell you to listen to me."

"This is absurd," Theo threw his arms up in disgust. "How does he get away with murdering someone like that?"

"I couldn't tell you," Alice frowned. "Makes you really wonder though," she mumbled, "about Mom...?"

"Are you suggesting—"

"Implying," Alice cut him off. "I'm not accusing or blaming anyone. It just seems convenient with his sudden call to arms before she died."

"He wouldn't—he couldn't have," Theo tried to rationalize. "She wouldn't have been allowed in his war room."

"It has nothing to do with her being in there," Alice shook her head. "Mom was the queen for one reason. Remember?"

"She was a queen to the people," Theo answered. "So what?"

"The people are suffering, Theo!" Alice burst out. "She knew that *he* knew. But how do you justify a war if your people are dying at home? Her voice stood in his way and the only way he could get his plans through was to silence the people. *Her* people. *Our* people."

"It can't be true," Theo tried to deny. Deep down he knew she was right, everything lined up.

"Believe me or not," Alice deflated, "it makes no difference to me. No one would believe me anyway."

Theo felt the guilt twist in his chest. "It's been a long day," he said as he tried to turn himself off the bed. He got his legs to limply roll off the side so he could sit. Then with as much might as he could muster, he pulled himself to his feet.

"Just—everything we talked about in here..." Alice said sheepishly.

"I don't know what you're talking about," Theo answered before she could complete her sentence.

"Be careful, Theo," Alice called to him as he moved the chair from behind the door and swung it open.

"I will," Theo nodded as he left the room.

He stepped out into the hallway, closing the door behind him. It was dark outside the room except for the little bit of light that was coming from underneath Alice's doors. He felt nervous standing out in the open alone. It felt like something was stalking him from the shadows.

"You're just overthinking," he mumbled to himself. Taking a deep breath, he started walking across the castle grounds, back towards his bedchamber.

Something about the quiet air in the castle gave Theo goosebumps. He could feel the hair on his neck standing on end and every step he took was methodically placed to make as little noise as he could.

When he cautiously turned the first corner, he slammed chest to chest with a guard on patrol. The prince crashed to the ground and landed hard on his back.

"Ali—Your Highness!" The guard quickly panicked and sprang to his feet.

Theo got up and dusted himself off. "I'm sorry," he said looking down at his feet embarrassed. "I wasn't paying attention to where I was going—"

"I know I could take you if I had the chance," the guard chuckled.

Theo looked up at the guard and he quickly recognized the face.

"Oli?" Theo smiled.

"I was wondering if I would run into you making a midnight snack run or something," the guard smiled back. He took off his helmet revealing the familiar dark-skinned young man with a similar mop of dark brown hair on top of his head. The sides of his hair were shaved down, the top was longer, and he kept everything in a neat bun. The slightly pointed tips of his ears protruded from the side of his head as they slipped out of his helmet.

Theo had never noticed Oli's ears. They were always tucked beneath his long hair.

"What are you doing here?" Theo asked him, surprised to see his friend.

Theo started to remember the training they did together.

The two of them were at the top of their division, but in skill and academically, Oli was the superior of the two.

"I've finally made my way into service," Oli answered proudly. "They were very impressed with my reputation and I was given a chance to show my skill. A couple of sword swings later, one headless sparring dummy, and a double arrow shot, I was promoted to the royal guard. Tonight is my first watch."

"So *you're* guarding the castle now? Boy, do I feel safer already," he teased, giving Oli a light shoulder punch. He wasn't going to admit it out loud, but Theo did feel safer knowing his old friend was watching over him. "Say, you wouldn't happen to be looking for anything else to do other than wander the castle all night, would you?" Theo asked.

"Well, considering that's all I'm supposed to be doing," Oli rolled his eyes playfully. "I can't leave my post."

"What if you didn't have to?" Theo smirked.

Oli gave him a skeptical glare.

"Guardsman Olsdeyr," Theo mockingly put on his diplomat's voice, "I order you to stand watch over my chambers this evening while I rest."

"Did you just—"

"Give an order to a royal guard?" Theo cut Oli off, "yes, I sure did."

"Fair enough," Oli shrugged. He took his helmet and slid his head back inside of it, carefully tucking the tips of his ears into the helmet.

Theo started walking down the corridor and Oli marched in tandem with him. The two talked the entire way. Sharing stories from the past few years while they were apart. Tales of their adventures, accounts of what they claimed were occasions of true love, and at one point Oli went on a rambling tangent about what the future held for him.

Eventually, the two boys reached the prince's chambers. Theo opened the door and Oli walked in behind him.

"You can leave your armor at the door if you like," Theo offered.

"No, Your Highness," Oli declined. "It's bad enough I'm in here while I'm supposed to be on duty. At least if I get caught, I'd like to look prepared."

"Fair enough," Theo shrugged as he wandered over towards his bed.

He noticed the saber propped against the bedpost. The women who patched him up earlier must have left it there. He grabbed the weapon and relocated it at the head of the bed.

"So what happened to the face?" Oli asked, catching Theo off guard.

"What?" Theo frowned.

"You know," Oli said, drawing a circle with his finger over his own face.

"Oh, that," Theo chuckled nervously. He'd forgotten his face was still scarred. "I—uh—had a little mishap on the stairs coming into the castle earlier," he lied. "I caught the last stair and went face first onto the stone."

"And it split you open like that?" Oli raised his eyebrow skeptically.

"Yeah," Theo nodded. "There was a bit of a sharp corner in the cobblestone and you know my luck, I snagged my nose on it."

He could tell Oli didn't buy it, the lack of response made Theo nervous.

"It's really nothing. Kick your boots off and relax a little," Theo deflected. He gestured towards the adjacent sitting couch that was between his bed and the balcony arches.

"I shouldn't," Oli shook his head.

"Your prince demands it," Theo joked.

Oli rolled his eyes and made his way over to the couch. He unclipped his sword and sheath from his belt and placed it against the arm. Reaching over his shoulder, he pulled the pointed shield off his back and set it against the sword. Then with a huge sigh of relief, Oli fell back onto the chair and sank into the pillows. It was a little uncomfortable having his armor on but it was nice to get off his feet for a minute.

The two trailed off into more stories. They talked for hours and it felt like no time had passed since the last they saw each other.

"It's been quite some time, hasn't it?" Oli laughed as he tucked his hands behind his head. "How's your sister been?"

Theo made a face at the ceiling when he heard the question. "I'm sorry?"

"It's been a while—"

"No, the thing about my sister?"

"I was just curious about how she is. What's she been up to since last we talked?" Oli said, carefully choosing his words.

"I don't know," Theo shrugged. "She's probably looking for a husband or something. The king won't give her the crown, so the next best thing in my opinion is to leave. Honestly, I don't blame her."

"Has she met with anyone?" Oli asked as he stiffened a little.

Theo could hear his armor as he adjusted. "Don't think so. At least nobody I'm aware of." Theo rolled onto his side. "Why are you so worried about my sister?"

Oli tilted his head up, looking at Theo, "It's my job and sworn duty to worry about your family."

Theo gave him a skeptical frown before rolling onto his back again.

As the night grew older and the constellations in the midnight sky began to shine through the arches, the two boys drifted to sleep.

MOTHER'S NIGHTMARE

Theo hoped having Oli nearby while he slept would distract him from his thoughts, but his dreams refused to forget.

In a deep sleep that felt like it might never break, Theo dreamt of himself and his father locked in battle. Sword duels, military conquests, and even a bare-knuckled fistfight. Every time he lost and every time he was pulled into the next violent dream.

He could feel his heart about to burst from his chest but it wasn't enough to wake him. His body was too exhausted to respond to anything and needed rest. His face still ached, his legs burning, and his arms were heavy.

"Theo," a familiar voice echoed in his head.

"Mom?" Theo called out, sitting up in his dream state.

"Theo," his mother's sweet voice filled his ears again.

It struck a chord in the prince's chest. More than a week had passed since he last heard her voice and it twisted his heart in knots.

"Where are you?" His words echoed into the empty air

around him. He found himself sitting in a field of grass in the north castle garden.

It had been ages since the garden was this lush and vibrant. The tall, sturdy tree that stood in the middle of the field wasn't gray and withered as he remembered. Green leaves bearing the biggest, darkest plums Theo had ever seen shook in the breeze.

"Theo," the Queen's voice whistled in his ears through the wind.

"I'm here, Mom!" Theo answered with childish excitement up towards the orange sky.

The wind raged, shaking the plums from the tree and they fell from withering branches as the leaves shriveled into dust.

In a single blink, everything began to decay before his eyes. The plums molded and crumbled into the grass. Any leaves that parted from the tree turned to ash before they hit the ground.

Theo's chest began to pound and ache. It felt like his heart was about to leap from his body. He put his hands on his chest to stop his heart from escaping but when he looked down, his body was withering into the same black ash.

Everything around him was swallowed by darkness, an empty abyss Theo had anticipated. Endlessly floating around with nothing but your conscious thoughts.

He started to notice there wasn't a floating sensation. He was sitting in a chair. But not just any chair... his father's throne.

Panic filled the prince's body as he looked up at the Grand Hall that housed the throne.

It was empty.

No banners hung from the pillars that lined the imported granite floors. The small wooden chairs that typically lined the long matching table at the foot of the throne's podium were deserted. No generals, governors, or dignitaries discussing business or sharing stories stood around the hall. Not even a single guard was to be found.

But for being an empty room, he watched something with awe. A floating orb of light.

It was blinding white with wisps of blue painting the end of the light flares that spawned off its surface.

Gradually, the orb floated closer and closer to the prince. The light didn't divert from a straight path and Theo watched it come towards him.

As the orb hovered at the base stair leading up to the throne's parapet, it began to materialize into a human figure. Building from the bottom, two legs began walking up the steps. Piece by piece a body was formed until standing in front of Theo was his mother, clear as day.

"Mom!" He shouted as he threw his arms out and around her neck. But something caught him in the ribs.

It was painful, he realized with delay. He didn't know why it was impossible to scream. He fought his hardest but something covered his face. He couldn't breathe and was starting to suffocate.

"Theo, honey," his mother spoke to him.

His eyes focused and he saw his mother letting go of a black dagger that was protruding from his abdomen.

His mind went blank. He was in total shock as he continued fighting to breathe. The handless dagger drove deeper into his ribs and his lungs started to burn.

"Theo." His mother's voice was stern and commanding. "Theo, listen to me, honey. You need to wake up."

"I'm dying," he choked out involuntarily.

"That's why you need to wake up!" she shouted at him.

"But you did this to me," Theo grunted through the suffocating pain.

"Theo, this isn't real," his mother sorrowfully croaked. "Wake up! Wake up and fight!"

The dagger's tip pierced his lung, jolting him from his sleep with white-hot agony.

His eyes burst open and he tried to sit up but he was forced back into the bed. His vision started to clear and he saw the dark figure with its hand tightly over his face.

He fought to see who or what it was but a hood and a black mask hid their face. He struggled against the suffocating hand as his vision started to fade to a pinhole.

Flexing every muscle in his body, he felt the cold sting of the blade inside his abdomen. He couldn't see the dagger but he knew that it was deep into his lower rib cage.

"My saber," his mother's voice whispered in his ear.

Theo struggled against the hooded figure but to no avail.

"My saber!" she said again, her voice shaking in fear.

Theo tried to get his arm free from beneath his assailant.

"Stop moving you little shit!" The hooded figure grunted through the mask. Two bloodshot, brown eyes peered from inside the hood with dark circles and bags underneath. "The king wants you dead!"

Theo's arm came free and he managed to get his fingers under the mask. He pulled the ceramic face from the hood and a man's face was illuminated by the moonlight. He looked like he hadn't slept in days. The bloodshot and dark eyes didn't blink. A strong smell of burnt spices and booze wafted from the man.

"Just give up already!" the man snarled into Theo's face. "You need to die!"

Theo pulled his arm in and elbowed the man square in the nose.

The man's hand slipped off Theo's mouth and he gasped for air. He pushed and pulled himself out from under the man, but didn't get far.

The man grabbed Theo by the throat and forced him back into the bed.

"Who—are—you?" Theo choked out with his last bit of breath.

"Shut up!" the man growled.

Theo felt the blade in his abdomen slide out of the wound. The tip of the unseen blade grazed the skin across the middle of his lower chest before piercing into the side of his ribs. He felt the blade dig deep.

"Stop!" Theo begged through a helpless scream.

"You're just as worthless as those street scum you love so much," the man sneered as he gripped around Theo's throat tightly.

Theo's vision started fading to black again. He could see stars and felt a blood vessel about to burst inside his eye. *This was it*, he thought as his muscles gave out and couldn't fight any longer.

As Theo accepted his fate, something being shattered rang in his ears.

The hands around his throat released and the hooded man fell off the side of the bed.

Theo gasped for air as his vision came back to him and he scrambled to the other side of the bed to get as far from the assassin as he could get.

Standing at the foot of the bed was Oli holding the remaining pieces of a shattered vase.

Before either of them could say anything to each other, the assassin grabbed Oli's leg and pulled it out from under him. With a clatter of armor, Oli hit the stone floor and let out a pained grunt. The assassin pulled himself off the floor, using the bedposts to stabilize himself.

"Elves," the man spat in disgust as he pulled his mask back over his face. "And you're not even satisfying enough to be a trophy, nasty half-breed."

A storm of fire filled Theo's chest as he watched the man move over Oli and spit on him.

He wanted to leap over the bed and strangle the man but there was still a dagger protruding from his ribs. The sudden realization of the burning pain in his side flooded over him, throwing him into a cold sweat.

The man across the bed reached beneath his cloak and pulled out another matching dagger.

"No!" Theo tried to cry out but nothing more than an exhausted, airy breath escaped his lips.

"I think I'll take your ears before I kill you," the man snarled as he knelt down with the dagger behind the bed frame.

Without a single thought, Theo ripped the dagger from his rib cage and threw it at the man before he disappeared behind the mattress.

The bloody blade caught the hooded man in the back of the shoulder.

"Damnit!" the man shouted as he stumbled towards the door.

Theo stumbled his way around the bed using it as a crutch. He came around to the other side and found Oli laying on the ground.

"Oli," Theo grunted. "Oli, wake up!"

"I'm alive," Oli groaned as he blinked at the prince.

Theo tried to kneel down and help him up but the pain in his sides burned. "Gahwk!" Theo choked.

Oli sprang to his feet and caught Theo as he collapsed forward. He threw Theo's arm over his shoulders and started helping him to the door.

"No, wait—" Theo grunted through the pain. "My mother's —saber—"

"We need to get you help," Oli argued.

"I—need—it," Theo gasped.

Oli closed his eyes and let out a quick sigh. "If you die on this wall—"

"I'm not going to die," Theo weakly tried to assure him. But the pain was unbearable and he wasn't so sure if he believed himself.

Oli carefully propped Theo against the door frame inside the room and rushed to retrieve the saber. He ran back around to the other side of the bed to pick up his weapons and helmet, securing the sheathed sword on his hip and shield on his back.

He grabbed Theo again, propping his arm over his shoulder, and dragged him out of the room. He carried Theo down the corridor as fast as he could but between the full suit of armor and the wounded prince they had to stop at the first turn.

"We can't—stop," Theo winced at the pain of trying to stand on his own.

"I know," Oli panted for air. "This is a lot harder than it looks. Getting knocked on your ass in a full suit of metal armor isn't the best feeling."

"I—know—" Theo choked out. "We need—to find—Alice."

"Your sister?" Oli stood up straight and started loading Theo over his shoulders again.

"She—can help—us," Theo said.

"But so can the nurses," Oli argued.

"We can't—trust anyone," Theo shook his head in defeat. "That assassin—was sent by—" There was no air left in his lungs. "I can't—" he gasped. His lungs were on fire and he could feel his throat swelling shut.

"Okay, okay," Oli nodded nervously. "Your sister it is." He tried not to hurt Theo as he repositioned him to make him easier to carry.

The two boys hobbled through the castle, avoiding being seen by ducking into the shadows to evade the guards on patrol.

Theo's pain was excruciating and every so often Oli had to

put a hand over his mouth to get him to be quiet as guards wandered past.

When they made it to Alice's chambers, Oli knocked on the iron-trimmed oak doors.

No answer.

He knocked harder, the banging echoing down the halls.

Still nothing.

"Princess, please open the door—".

"There he is!" A man's voice shouted from down the corridor. Three knights began charging towards them with their swords out. "Halt where you are, assassin!" the lead knight shouted.

Theo recognized the man's voice. Then he recognized the knight's armor. But before he could piece the two together, he was yanked by his collar and thrown into Alice's chamber.

ALICE AND OLSDEYR

The two boys went painfully crashing onto the floor on the other side of the massive doors. Alice stood over them as the doors slammed shut behind her.

Oli scrambled to his feet and braced his shoulder against the doors.

"What happened?" Alice burst out as she knelt down next to her brother.

"He was attacked, Your Highness," Oli answered.

"Drop the formalities, Oli. Who's after you?" Alice clipped.

She placed her hands gently against Theo's sides. He hardly noticed the pain as she applied pressure to his ribs because he was suffocating on his own throat and his lungs screamed for air. He was in pure agony.

"I was with your brother when he was attacked in his chambers. An assassin got into his room and stabbed him. I think the dagger had a poisoned blade."

"Is that who's on the other side of—"

"Open the door in the name of the king!" An angry voice came from the other side of the door.

"Guards?" Alice looked up confused.

"His Majesty's knights—to be more specific," Oli grunted as the knights slammed against the door. "I don't mean to offend, my lady—" Oli strained out, "but is there a barricade to this—"

Alice raised a hand and the spiraled-iron trim of the wooden doors glinted with a white hue before fading back to normal. Oli hesitated to step back but when he saw the door wouldn't budge, he eased against the wood.

"The doors are sealed, be useful and pull me some of the Goat's Beard from the balcony," Alice demanded.

"Goat's Beard?" Oli mumbled to himself as he ran out onto the balcony. "I don't see a goat out here!" He called from outside the chamber.

"It's a plant—never mind," Alice rolled her eyes. "Little green leaves—look like teardrops—thin stems."

Oli searched around the balcony but didn't know what she was describing.

"Did you find it?" Alice shouted from inside.

"You have so many plants!" Oli shot back anxiously.

Theo felt something building in his mouth and Alice watched as a white foam bubbled in the corners of Theo's purple lips.

"Dammit Olsdeyr, this isn't time for jokes!" Alice snapped.

"I'm not joking!" Oli clipped. "You have dozens of plants out here!"

"It's in the far right corner as you come out through the doors. Little teardrop on a thin vine. I need ones that have purple tips."

"Now they're purple—" Oli was cut off by the slamming coming from the door.

The knights began battering against the door with a heavy object trying to break it down.

Oli reset himself in the doorway and looked around the right side of the balcony.

There it was, tangled around a pillar of the wall. He raced to the pillar and began pinching off as many of the little leaves he could get between his thumbs and index fingers. "Found it!"

"Great, I need a good amount of that," Alice answered. "Once you've got that—Theo!"

The prince began to convulse on the floor. His body was shaking as his eyes rolled back into his head.

"Damnit, damnit, damnit!" Alice cursed under her breath. She got up from beside her brother and rushed out onto the balcony. Swiftly on her toes, she grabbed a long vine of the purple-tipped, teardrop leaves from the pillar, plucked a white root from another pot, and scooped a small bit of soil from the pink and white flowers at the door. She threw all the ingredients into a stone mortar and began crushing it with a small wooden pestle. Grinding the bits and pieces together, she quickly carried the bowl back out into the balcony and picked several bright red berries that dangled from the stone parapet that bordered the end of the balcony.

When the berries mixed into the dry powder and made a paste, Alice rushed to her brother's side and started applying the red mixture to his wounds.

Theo felt all the pain being drawn from his body and out of his wounds. The burning faded and his throat released, allowing him to gasp for all the air his lungs could take. The foam in his mouth tasted like bile and left a nasty feeling in his stomach. Blood rushed back into his face and lips as he turned on his side before vomiting on the floor.

When he turned back and saw his sister leaning over him, he wrapped his arms around her shoulders.

"H—he did it," Theo stuttered weakly into her shoulder, trying not to cry. "He sent an assassin. It was the knight from the street."

Alice carefully helped Theo to his feet, barely able to help hold him up. "Oli, please—" She grunted as she offered her brother over to him.

He did as requested and took Theo over his shoulder again.

"You two won't get far with him like that," Alice thought aloud as she turned and went to the dresser where she'd stashed the potion that calmed Theo earlier. She clanked a few glass bottles around before pulling out a small round bottle that glimmered red from within.

At first, Oli thought it was an apple, but as she came closer with it, he could see the contents were liquid.

"You're going to have to give him this in doses," Alice started to explain. "That paste I put on his wounds needs time to clear the poison from his body and must be washed off before you let him drink more than half of this bottle. Otherwise, his wounds might heal with the poisoned paste." She walked over and knocked on a door that was next to the dresser. She didn't wait for a response but instead opened it and walked into the room behind it.

Oli heard a muffled conversation coming from the room. He couldn't make out what they were saying over the banging on the other door.

He started scanning for an escape route. One where he could protect the prince if the door suddenly burst open.

Alice returned to the room again and behind her was a younger woman not much younger than Theo. She was putting on a dark cloak that covered her blue and white nightgown.

"Ashti is going to guide you from here," Alice instructed a now confused Oli.

"What? Where are we going?" Oli protested. "Once he's good, you two can just tell the guards that we're okay and to find the assassin now loose in the castle! They could be going for your father—"

"Those men *are* the assassins," Alice snapped. "Those are the men—the king sent them to kill Theo!"

Oli stood there, stunned.

"There's no time for this," Alice clipped, "you two are leaving the castle and then you're leaving the kingdom. Ashti will get you to your first waypoint. From there she'll explain the rest."

"Your Highness—"

Alice placed a hand on Oli's cheek. "In another life—" she choked on her words and tried to smile through the tears pooling in her eyes. "In another life, maybe I could have kept you by my side. But our destinies now lie in different directions."

Oli swallowed hard. "I will see you again, cross my heart," he promised her.

"I will count the days until we see each other again," Alice said through the knot in her throat. "Your duty is to my brother and *your* friend," She shook her head and swallowed hard. "You need to go. Get him out of—"

Oli leaned over and planted a kiss on Alice's lips. It was quick and subtle. As Oli pulled away, Alice followed, trying to hold the moment as it vanished too quickly.

"When I return, my princess," Oli began as he started shuffling the prince towards Ashti, "we will finish this moment."

Without another glance, Oli, Theo, and Ashti ducked into the other room and vanished.

Alice turned towards the door where the banging persisted. She raised her hand and the iron trimming glowed white once again. The doors burst open and four Knights tumbled onto the floor.

Alice dropped to her knees and began to weep.

ASHTI THE BRAVE

Oli turned, with Theo hanging on his shoulders as they both stumbled after Ashti.

She drew her cloak's hood over her head and pulled on a book in the bookshelf against the left wall. The shelf slid along the stone, revealing a tunnel with an unlit torch mounted in the wall. Ashti took the handle from the metal ring and held it in front of her face.

"This way," she whispered as she pinched the cloth-wrapped end of the torch with her thumb and index finger. There was a spark and a fire flicked from the now burning torch.

Oli did a double-take but it didn't help. He knew what he had just seen and couldn't believe it.

Ashti didn't wait for questions and turned into the tunnel with her torch held high.

Oli did his best to keep up with her pace, but between his armor and the prince suffering on his shoulders, he kept stopping to adjust.

"Wait here," Ashti said softly, "we need to give him some of my lady's potion. You're not going to be able to carry him the rest of the way. It's just going to slow us down."

"I'll carry him to my last dying breath if I must," Oli grunted as he propped Theo against the wall and pulled out the apple-like bottle of red liquid. He uncorked it and pressed it to the prince's mouth.

Theo took a huge gulp and tried to go for a second but Oli pulled the bottle away. It soothed his throat and gave him a warm feeling in his chest that reminded him of the mead served at festivals and ceremonies in the castle.

When the liquid hit his stomach, his whole body tingled. The pounding between his ears started to settle and his aching muscles were loosening.

"How do you feel?" Oli asked him.

"I would—feel a lot better—" Theo grunted. "If I could finish that."

"No, Your Highness," Oli shook his head, feeling an uncomfortable tingle in his neck as he denied a member of the royal family, "Alice told me—"

"We need to move," Ashti cut in. "They're going to find us soon if we don't. Can you walk?" she asked Theo.

He tried to push off of the wall, but he stumbled like a foal taking its first steps and crashed against the opposite wall.

"I can carry you still—" Oli moved to help.

Theo shook his head. "Don't carry me," he grunted, trying to suppress the lingering pain, "but I will need a crutch."

"I've got you," Oli said as he helped his friend stand.

The three of them continued down the tunnel as it turned and spiraled. Ashti held a decent distance from the two boys, occasionally stopping to let them catch up before she would scout ahead again.

After a long walk, the tunnel came to a dead end.

"What's this?" Oli burst out.

"Keep your voice down!" Ashti whispered intensely.

"But we're trapped," Oli argued, lowering his tone.

"Shh!" Ashti glared at him. She turned back to the wall and ran her hand along the grooves.

Oli grew impatient and was about to scream at her again when the stone wall split in two and opened outwards like a door.

Moonlight poured into the tunnel and a hole led to the western valley outside the castle walls.

"Where are you taking us?" Oli grunted as he bounced Theo further up his shoulder for better leverage.

"My lady instructed me to take you to the Tankard Knight. It's a tavern in the lower quarter of the city. We're meeting someone there," Ashti explained as she moved into the night air.

Oli pulled out the bottle of red liquid and poured more down Theo's throat.

After a couple of seconds, Oli could feel Theo beginning to bear his own weight. He left his arm out as the prince cautiously let go of him and stepped down the steep hill.

"You got it?" Oli asked.

"Y—yeah," Theo grunted, "I think I can walk a bit. But stay close, I don't know how long of a walk it will be."

"I've got you, Your Highness," Oli nodded.

The two boys followed Ashti through the tall, wispy grass. They trudged over a tall hill that formed the ditch at the end of the western valley where Ashti stopped and turned.

"We're almost to the—" She froze, staring past the boys.

They both spun around and saw at the bottom of the hill were three armored knights climbing the steep incline. Their boots sank into the soft soil that held tightly to each step they took. But they kept moving.

"Don't stop!" Theo commanded as he turned and hobbled up the last part of the hill. Oli and Ashti hesitated before following the prince's lead.

The three of them crested the horizon and were met by the flickering lamplight glowing off the town.

There were people out and about walking through the streets. Some dragging along restless children, others carrying sacks or baskets, and many more people strolling about the late night.

"We'll have cover if we cut through the streets," Ashti said. "Pull your hood—" She stopped, this time staring at them both. Without a word, she unfastened the brooch of her cloak and pulled it from her shoulders. She neatly balled it in her hands and thrust it into Theo's hands.

"What are you going to hide with?" Theo asked as he pushed the cloak back at her. "I'll be fine. Nobody has seen me."

"They've all seen you," Ashti pleaded with her eyes, "and you need to take this off!" She reached for the top of his head and before he could flinch, she jumped up to pluck the golden crown from his head. "That will only make you more noticeable."

She turned and looked up at Oli. "Take him to the Tankard Knight. You'll know the place. It has a little sign over the door. When you arrive, give this to the innkeeper. When the time comes, someone will come for you."

Ashti pulled herself onto the tips of her toes, Oli bent down, and she whispered into his ear. He nodded along, listening intently.

Oli straightened out and Ashti lowered herself.

"From there you two will be safe—"

"Stop!" A voice called out from behind them.

"Go!" Ashti shouted. She grabbed them both by the sleeves and threw herself in front of the three advancing knights.

"We're not—" they both protested, but they suddenly weren't next to her at all. They were inside the town. Far out in the shadowy distance, a small dark figure faced down three much larger beasts.

The largest had a shield on their arm and swung it at the smaller figure. Both of them went flying in opposite directions with a flash that was quickly followed by an echoing bang that flooded the streets. The larger being didn't get up. One of the two knights still standing moved towards their fallen member while the other one advanced on Ashti's figure as she got to her feet.

A flash of fire swallowed the advancing figure leaving nothing behind seconds later. The final knight rushed Ashti in an animalistic fury. She was nearly obliterated but her figure seemed to shift around the knight.

The charging buffoon tumbled forward and crashed head-first into the ground. But Ashti didn't see the first knight getting back to their feet behind her.

They drew a long sword from their hip and thrust the blade through Ashti's back.

Theo wanted to scream out and run to help her, but Oli grabbed him by the arm and pulled him further into the city.

"Let me go!" Theo demanded as he tried to break loose from Oli. But his strength wasn't enough. Oli moved Theo into a crowd of people watching a street performer juggle.

"Your High—Theo," Oli corrected himself, "we have to keep moving."

Theo felt a burning anger building in the pit of his stomach. "We're just going to leave her dead in that field?" He snapped under his breath, trying not to draw attention to them. "That's horrible and inhumane. We need to recover her—find her medical treatment. We could save her life. She was innocent in all this—"

Oli shifted directions and ducked into a dark alley. He spun Theo around, shoved his back against a wall, and lifted him by the scruff of his shirt. "Shut up and listen to me! You're in danger and both my job and hers is to protect you at all costs. She laid down her life for you and I am willing to do the same. You need to understand that in times like this when you're—*we're* being hunted, sacrifices and losses are going to happen. I don't like it any more than you. It's horrifying and not easy to choke down but you have to. At the moment a lot is at stake."

Theo was taken by surprise at being manhandled. In all his life he had never been touched or shoved. Oli's words cut him deep but he wouldn't argue.

"Look," Oli calmed down, releasing the prince's collar, "if you want to survive whatever we're doing, you've got to put your emotions aside. Don't look back. Do you understand?"

Theo felt a familiar calm to his emotions. Like when his sister gave him a calming potion. He wanted to burst at Oli for handling him so roughly but there was nothing inside him to project it.

"I'm going to step out of this alley to stand guard while you put that on," Oli said looking down at the bundled cloak in Theo's hands. "When you're ready, we're going to make our way through the streets until we find the tavern—"

Theo placed a hand on Oli's shoulder and looked him in the eye. "When we come back home, I want to commemorate her and preserve her memory."

Oli was taken back by the request.

"Remind me, I want to build her a statue in my mother's garden. As my closest—my *only* friend, I tell you this in confidence so that you will make sure I uphold my promise."

"I understand," Oli nodded.

THE TANKARD KNIGHT

Oli turned back towards the street and stopped at the end of the alley. He looked down at his guard's armor and started unbuckling the chest piece.

Theo wanted to say something but he understood.

Oli placed the chest armor on the ground in the alley along with his shield. He refastened his belt and adjusted his sword on his hip. "You're going to need these for right now," he said as he knelt down and pulled out two daggers from the sides of his boots. He turned and offered them to the prince.

Theo took the daggers and bounced them in his hands, feeling the weight of the blades. He tucked the daggers into his belt and threw the cloak over his shoulders, clasping it around his neck. As he pulled his hood up, he stared at the crown in his other hand.

Oli stepped out into the busy street as a cart pushed through the crowds and motioned for Theo to follow.

Theo took the crown and hooked it on his belt beside one of the daggers. With a deep sigh, he pulled the hood further over his face and went into the street.

"Follow me, stay close, and don't talk to anyone," Oli instructed.

Theo nodded and they pushed on through the crowds. They ducked into alleys trying to avoid being seen by guard patrols.

"Oli, we need to find somewhere to hide," Theo groaned as he began to lose faith, "or get out of the kingdom—"

Oli spun around and glared at him. "Keep your voice down," he clipped through his teeth.

Theo stiffened uncomfortably as something caught his eye. "We're here," he mumbled, pointing at the sign hanging past Oli's shoulder.

Oli spun around and saw the wood-carved sign shaped like an upside-down knight's helmet filled with ale.

Oli started towards the sign and Theo followed him into the tavern. Inside was busy and they managed to sneak through without being noticed. Oli found the most inconspicuous table in the back and Theo sat facing the door.

"You stay here," Oli said, not sitting with Theo. "I'm going to go get us a drink."

Theo frowned. "This isn't a time—"

Oli turned and walked across the tavern, ignoring the prince.

Theo leaned forward resting his elbows against the table and scanned the room.

Every other table was surrounded by three or four beings, some of the likes Theo had never seen before. There were people with pointed ears like Oli's and a few burly beings with thick, braided beards. At one point he could have sworn he saw a man with horns and a pointed demon's tail.

As he continued scanning, he locked eyes with an older man with hollow cheeks sitting at the bar. Theo quickly averted his attention to the floor hoping the man didn't notice but he could feel them still staring.

Oli pushed his way to the bar and patiently waited until the large man behind the bar stopped in front of him.

"Whatcha havin'?" the burly, broad-chested man with long white hair and a trimmed beard to match asked. He looked like he'd seen a fight or two, maybe even some battle. His muscles stretched the sleeves of his shirt so tight, the slightest touch of a blade could split the fabric.

"Um—yeah," Oli answered nervously, "two house ales, please."

The man nodded, grabbed two tankards from under the counter, and turned to the keg situated in the wall. A couple of seconds later, he spun back around and set two foaming tankards in front of Oli.

"That's four copper," the man's deep voice boomed in Oli's ears over the noisy tavern ambiance.

Oli reached into his pocket and plucked out six brownish coins from his pocket, dropped them in the man's hand, and then pulled out the piece of paper Ashti gave him before they were separated.

The man pocketed the coins and unfolded the slip. He scanned it for a moment before crumpling it in his hand and giving Oli a nod. "Sit tight. I'll have Mae bring you some food."

Oli was confused but he returned the nod nervously and took the tankards. He went back to the table and noticed that Theo had his face tucked into his chest.

"What's wrong?" Oli asked softly as he placed the drinks in front of the prince.

"There's someone at the bar who's been staring at me the entire time. We looked right at each other," Theo mumbled from behind his hood.

Oli glanced over his shoulder but didn't see anyone looking in their direction. "There's nobody there."

Theo hesitantly lifted his head and saw the person was no

longer there. "I swear they were staring at—"

"Is this the table expecting a couple of snacks?" a stout woman in a long, green and white skirt asked as she set down a wooden platter with cuts of dried meats, sausages, cheeses, and bread. She had a mane of curly orange hair that bounced with every step. She leaned over to Oli and whispered, "You'll have to hang tigh'. Yer contact is delayed." She straightened herself and walked back into the crowd.

The two boys exchanged confused looks. They sat in the tavern and didn't say a word to each other for a long while. Theo quaffed the ale the best he could. It was cold and soothed his sore throat. Between breathing and inhaling his drink, he picked most of the platter clean.

Oli nursed his drink anxiously while his attention was on the door. He scanned the faces of the room trying to get a read on anyone who should be avoided. He wouldn't raise his tankard past his nose.

When the two finished their drinks and the food was gone, the stout woman returned to clear everything.

"Would ya like somethin' else?" she asked with a warm smile.

"Do you have anything easier to swallow?" Theo asked through a mouth full of stale bread.

"Nothin' for that price," she said. "Is there somethin' in particular yer lookin' for?"

"Do you have any mead?" Theo shifted in his seat.

"That's very expensive stuff," the woman warned. "We only sell it by the bottle since hardly anyone can afford it."

Theo looked at Oli, trying to get his opinion on the matter but he was too focused on watching the groups behind the woman's shoulder.

"I'll take another one of these, please," Oli mumbled, blindly pointing at the empty tankard in the woman's hand.

She nodded and looked back at Theo. "D'ya still want the mead?"

Theo gave her a side frown and shook his head. "No, that's okay. I'll do another one of those too." He gestured to the tankards.

"Sure thing, sweetheart," the woman smiled. She stopped and leaned down next to Oli's ear again. "Yer contact is on the way. Make sure you have everyt'ing you need. There won' be a lotta time when they arrive."

Oli nodded and the woman wandered back behind the bar again.

"So, we just—" Theo mumbled, gesturing to the table.

"For now, yeah," Oli shrugged. He drew his attention to the prince, "I have no idea what we're waiting for. But he knew what the note meant, and she's been talking to us about it."

"Do you know who we're waiting for?" Theo asked softly, trying to avoid any eavesdroppers from hearing him.

Oli shook his head, "They're supposed to find us, I guess."

They sat quietly at the table for another long while, only speaking when the woman returned with fresh drinks and more food. She didn't say anything to Oli this time and made her way through the now dwindling pockets of the midnight crowd in the tavern.

"What if our contact isn't who we think it is?" Theo asked anxiously. "Maybe we missed them already. What are we going to do if—"

"Theo," Oli said dryly, "if they close the tavern, we can start thinking about that. Until then, just sit still and relax."

Time continued to pass and the tavern steadily emptied and the stout woman came back to refill their drinks until eventually, the two of them were all that was left in the tavern.

"Alrigh', boys," the woman said as she wandered back over to their table, "here's the deal, big guy over there is kickin' me outta here and tellin' me to get some rest. He's gonna stick around until you two are picked up, okay?"

"What happened to the contact?" Oli asked.

"Not sure," the woman frowned, "they were sendin' us messages but they've gone silen' the las' few hours."

Oli swallowed hard.

"Don' worry," the woman smiled, "t'ings like this happen. I'm sure whoever is suppos'd to meet ya is jus' laying low for a moment. Makin' sure dey're not bein' followed."

"How long is that going to take?" Theo asked.

"Dunno," the woman shrugged. "You could be here for a while. But don' you worry, Timour will take good care of you, I promise." She jutted a thumb over her shoulder towards the large man behind the bar. He was wiping down the keg taps with a rag and replacing them with large corks.

"Thank you," Oli said to the woman.

"Don' mention it," the woman laughed. "I'm sorry the princess wasn't able to be here. With all her planning and all."

"What?" Theo sat up. "What plan?"

"I'm sorry, dear," the woman sighed, "but that's not for me to explain. I need to get out of here before we attract attention. Maybe when Timour is done cleaning, he can explain."

She spun on her heels and waddled towards the bar again. She plucked a gray cloak from under the counter, threw it over her shoulders, and headed out of the tavern. "I give you all my prayers, boys!" she called as the door closed behind her.

There was nothing but the crackle of the fireplace in the now spacious tavern. The two boys sat quietly at their table, nursing the last bits of ale in their mugs. Timour occasionally made a grunting noise or cleared his throat to break the ominous silence. Another hour or so passed and Theo began to get restless. He was about to stand and walk around when the front door of the tavern flew open.

IMPROVISING DESTINY

Theo and Oli froze in their seats as two cloaked figures walked through the open door. The first into the tavern was a number of heads shorter than the second one who locked the door behind them. Both of them with their hoods drawn over their faces.

At the bar, the smaller being climbed up onto a stool and began talking to Timour while the larger figure braced a chair to the door.

"Right, we're here for the princess," a man's voice came from the short figure on the stool.

"She's not here," Timour grunted with his fist wrapped in a rag that he used to wipe the tankards.

"What do you mean she's not here?" A woman's heavily accented voice came from the larger being. They pulled their hood back and revealed a dark-haired woman with long, pointed ears poking from the sides of her mane.

"I didn't ask," Timour shrugged, "but she sent someone in her place." He pointed across the tavern to the only occupied table. "They've been here all night waiting for you. I can't imagine how much longer the guards will take to finally track them here. What took you so long?"

"We got held up," the smaller being answered curtly. He pulled back the hood of his cloak and revealed himself as an older man. The man could hardly see over the stool before he climbed it, but he had the mature features of someone older than the king. White mutton chops cut through the middle of his cheeks and were separated by his bare, sharp chin.

Carefully the small man unclipped his cloak and pulled it from his shoulders. Strapped to his back was a loaded crossbow and his belt was lined with daggers. Theo grew nervous as he watched.

"We were on our way when a damn guard patrol raced past us to the castle. Couldn't risk getting caught so we ducked into the first place we could find—"

"*First* place we could find?" the woman with pointed ears snorted. "You dragged me three blocks into the parade of guards to hide out in a lady house."

"It was not—"

"Your chin was on the floor the entire time," the woman continued unraveling her companion's story. "I'd say I'm disgusted, but that doesn't do enough in this tongue to describe how much I want to hit you with—" she stopped and pursed her lips in frustration. "One of these!" She grabbed a chair and held it up at the small man, "the butt shelves!"

"You mean a chair?" the man snickered.

"Yeah," she nodded proudly. "I couldn't come up with the word. But that doesn't change the fact that I don't want to throw one at you any less than before!"

"If I had a gold piece for every time somebody said that to me, I'd be richer than a king," the man proclaimed with a smug smile.

"Then claim your riches so I can kill you with the chair and take it for myself—"

"Hi, yes, we're the ones Alice sent," Oli announced as he jumped from his seat and walked towards the bickering pair.

Theo remained frozen in his seat. He could feel one of the dagger pommels shoved in his belt shift uncomfortably beneath his ribs.

"We've got a tail on us and they've long-since killed our escort," Oli explained forwardly. "I'm sure it'll be no time before they find us here."

The man and the woman exchanged looks before bursting out in laughter.

"Oh boy," the man wheezed, "somebody thinks those scabs in shiny armor have the brainpower to track."

"Please, don't worry yourself," the woman smiled as she controlled her laughter. "No one will find you here. The streets are empty. It is—the dark time?"

"Night?" Oli answered confusedly.

"That one, night!" the woman bounced happily. "Please, forgive me. It's not my first language."

"I can tell, you do well with it." Oli nodded.

"Well I'll be," the man muttered, staring at Oli in astonishment, "an elf-kin in this kingdom?"

"What's elf-kin?" Oli frowned, shaking his head. "I'm not an elf. Both my parents were normal."

"*Normal*? I don't think that's true," the woman snorted. She reached up and touched the curve of Oli's ear but he jerked away from her hand.

"Are you trying to say my own parents lied to me?" Oli burst out. He wasn't sure why this made him so mad, but something was brewing in his head.

"That's more believable than the devil king allowing an elf among his people," the man shrugged. "Coulda been to protect you or something." He reached over his shoulder and swung his crossbow in front of his chest.

Oli positioned himself in front of Theo and started for his sword.

"Easy there, jumpy." The man threw a hand up defensively. "There's no need for that. I'm not gonna hurt you."

Oli froze, his hand still wrapped around the hilt of his sword.

"Look," the man sighed with an eye roll. He flourished his open hand in the air for a moment and the crossbow began to phase into a guitar. Like a mirage's illusion fading to reveal something entirely different.

"How did you—" Theo started to mumble

The man gave him a confused, yet concerned look. "I know this empire is a bit—tight on laws and such, but you can't tell me you've never seen a simple illusion spell."

Theo continued to stare at the man and his sudden guitar with astonishment. "My—my mother used to read me stories—fairy tales—fables—legends about magic. I never knew it was real."

"Real as you and me, yeah?" The man chuckled. He sat up in the barstool that was much too tall for him, tucked the guitar between his elbow and stomach, and with a single strum let out the most beautiful collection of notes Theo had ever heard. The man continued to play, changing the tune as he turned the white pegs at the head of the instrument. After a couple of seconds, he started to play softly.

Each note resonated in the empty tavern, bouncing off the walls and filling the whole room. Chills ran down the prince's spine and the hair on his neck stood on end. Theo couldn't believe that there could be music this beautiful.

The guitar itself wasn't anything impressive. It fit nicely against the man's small frame and he could reach every fret without an issue. On the edge where he rested his arm, it was smoothed and worn. There was obvious sun damage to the otherwise well-preserved wood. A couple of scratches and nicks here or there with varying depths. It looked like a well-loved instrument and the way he played each chord carried that feeling.

Theo watched in amazement as the man's fingers danced along the strings. At one point he even thought he saw the design in the wood begin to shift and move. The grain of the wood appeared to sway and move like waves in water. Circles and other shapes twinkled around dim-glowing runes as the notes went on.

Then the woman reached over and clasped her hand around the neck of the guitar, silencing the music.

"We don't have time for a concert," she said sternly, "we're already behind as it is. They're not going to pay us if we don't get out of the kingdom."

"She's right," Timour grunted from behind the bar. "Take those two and get them outta here before the king sends guards to toss the place. Mae might have my head if anything happens to this place."

"Are you two ready?" The woman asked, turning to Theo and Oli.

The boys were both frozen, waiting for the other to respond.

"We don't have all morning," the man pressured.

Oli nervously locked eyes with the woman, "The Hidden Sun sends her regards to the Lost Knight."

Everyone went stiff.

"We need to go, *now!*" the woman demanded as she pulled her hood over her head again.

"Do what she says," Timour said sternly to the boys. He started quickly moving from around the bar towards them.

"What's happening?" Theo asked Oli.

"Just stay calm, Your Highness," Oli commanded, trying to

heed his own words. He drew his sword from its sheath and stuck the blade between himself and Timour. "Don't take another step towards us until someone explains what's going on here. I'm all for getting out of here and especially out of this city for a while, but nobody is leading either of us out of here without at least an introduction."

"How do you know those words?" the small man barked.

"Somebody told me to say that to whoever came to get us," Oli answered. "She told me that's how I would know who was coming."

"That wasn't a rendezvous communication," the woman shook her head. "It's a coded message." She looked at Theo. "Your sister is in danger."

"How do you know my sister?" Theo stepped around the table and past Oli. He cautiously approached the woman.

"That is a much longer story than we have time for," she answered, "but how about this, my name is Nila. I was paid to help you flee the kingdom." She pointed to the smaller man, "his name is Jeb. He's my accomplice."

"Your sister hired us," Jeb explained shortly, "that's the important part there."

"What do you mean?" Oli straightened, lowering his sword slightly.

"Look, can we explain it on our way out? The sun is coming up soon and I'm sure the king will have his elites out after you," Jeb groveled as he climbed off the stool with his guitar on his back. He carefully walked closer to Oli with his hands raised cautiously. "There's no need for a fight right now. If you let us get you to safety, we will let you go your own path if you choose to. I'll even tell you everything if you make it to camp with us. The only caveat is you can't stay here."

Oli pulled his sword back up and turned the blade towards Jeb, halting his approach.

"Not another step," Oli threatened.

Jeb rolled his eyes and let out a deep sigh, "I'm sorry about this, kid. Tim?"

Before Oli could move out of reach from Timour's sudden grasp, Jeb swung his guitar around his neck, strummed a chord, and with a swirl of purple light, golden sparks scintillated off the strings into Oli's face. His eyes rolled back before completely closing and he collapsed into the massive tavernkeeper's arms.

"Nila, can you carry him?" Jeb asked, not looking at his partner.

"I don't think you've given me much choice," Nila sighed. She stepped away from the door and collected the now unconscious Oli over her shoulder. She reached down and pulled the red bottle from his belt. "Here," she said as she tossed it to Theo. "Wash that crap off you and drink the rest of this. You're going to need all of your strength."

"Wash—" Theo tried to get out but before he could finish, Jeb splashed him with the remainder of a drink left on a table. The yeasty smell flooded the prince's nose and soaked his clothes. "What are you doing—"

"Get yourself dried up and then drink all of that," Jeb instructed. He pulled a handkerchief from his pocket and threw it at Theo. "We're out of here once you're ready." Without another word, Jeb turned to the door and peeked through a window.

Theo frantically started scrubbing the now dried paste off his deep scabs. He looked up for a moment and watched Nila hobble across the tavern with Oli rag-dolled over her shoulder.

"What did you do to him?" Theo asked. His throat stung as he spoke. For the first time in the last few hours, he felt everything again. His joints ached, his head pounded, and his stomach growled. He tried his best to clean himself up and then downed the remaining red liquid.

The dreadful pains vanished as the concoction coated his throat. He watched as his scabs healed over, leaving only a lighter patch of skin to mark the wounds.

Jeb pulled his head back into the tavern, "Now's our best chance. Let's go."

Theo didn't have time to protest as Timour ushered him aggressively out the door.

Jeb and Nila with Oli in tow started up the street. They were moving at a quick pace and Theo struggled to keep up with them.

"Come on," Jeb growled with a whisper.

The sun was starting to peek through the alleys, leaving an orange glow to the horizon.

The church bells began to ring. Each strike felt like it would never end. After six rings the city went silent again. The occasional rooster's call echoed from a long distance yet there was no stir in the streets. Even the clicking sounds of the three sets of feet walking along the cobblestone were absent in the endless moment.

Theo began to grow uncomfortable with how calm it was.

They marched block after block, not turning or adjusting course once. After a while, they broke from the city borders and a short walk later took them to the main road that led straight out of the kingdom from the castle itself.

Jeb was only feet away from the road when the morning silence was broken by an eruption of horns coming from the castle.

Theo, Jeb, and Nila all snapped their attention at the front gate of the castle wall. The golden gates swung outward and a charge of guards on horseback burst onto the road towards the city. They broke off the road and through the grass to avoid running over the four of them at the turn.

Theo stood there frozen with his head down as the horses

stamped past. None of the guards paid them any mind as they kicked the dirt into the air. The last rider trotted closest to them and started handing sheets of parchment.

"From His Majesty," the guard spoke from inside their helmet.

Theo hesitantly looked up, blinded by the sun now poking over the guard's shoulder, and he reached out to take the parchment.

Before he could read it, the man heeled his horse and took off after the rest of the riders.

Theo's eyes quickly adjusted and he examined the parchment. His heart instantly plummeted in his stomach.

"Hey, guys," he mumbled at Jeb and Nila.

"We're almost out of here, hold on to it—"

"Prince George kidnapped!" A voice cried from within the city, cutting off Jeb's annoyed commands. "Elven infiltrator within the guard! Castle attacked in the night! Assassins captured! Elf on the run with the prince as hostage! Reward for the return of the prince and his captors!"

Theo's now wide eyes locked with Jeb's.

"Quickly," Jeb gritted through his teeth.

Theo leapt into a jog and chased after Jeb and Nila.

"Once we're beyond that treeline—" Nila grunted, still dragging Oli's body over her shoulders. "We're free—"

"Halt!" another voice called out. This one was a lot closer and heavy.

The three cautiously spun on their heels to face the looming figure being shadowed by the rising sun.

"The king has ordered the roads shut down," the heavy voice boomed as the figure approached. "The castle was under attack last night. We can't let anyone in or out until—"

"No, we completely understand," Jeb cut in.

Theo glanced over his shoulder. Expecting to look down at

Jeb, a hand touched his shoulder, and a much taller man pushed around the prince.

He had a sharp black beard with his long black hair pulled back into a knot on top.

"There's just the small issue of us getting home," the man spoke to the guard with Jeb's voice.

Theo blinked with confusion. He looked back again, this time at Nila. She shot him a warning glare and pursed her lips like she was going to shush him.

A chill ran down Theo's spine, causing him to straighten.

"We're from the farmlands on the southern plains. We came into the city for a little fun last night and someone got a little too excited." He jerked his thumb over his shoulder at Oli.

The shadowed figure leaned to the right, looking around the man with Jeb's voice, and then stood straight again.

"Harvest is coming up and we're starting the field prep today. Have to get the plows sharpened and the oxen groomed—"

"That will have to wait," the guard bellowed, "the kingdom is under lockdown by decree of the king. To let you leave would be to defy my king. Treason, punishable by death."

"Come on, friend," the man urged, his voice seeming to change the tone.

Theo still heard Jeb's voice, but something about how the words carried into his ears relaxed him. His anxieties calmed and he felt his own guard lowering.

"You can search any of us," the man offered with his arms out, "all we came here to do was have a few drinks in town before the harvest starts. Can't you just—"

The figure stepped closer to the man. A large, armored humanoid stepped into view and looked down on him.

"I could have you executed," the armored man threatened. His tone was bone-chilling and hushed. He leaned over the man, who was taller than Theo, and started moving his hands towards his belt.

"Well you're going to wish you had after this," the man shrugged.

In a blink of an eye, Theo watched as the man began to shrink, his clothes changing with his size, and there, standing between the armored man's legs, was Jeb.

Before the guard even drew his weapon, Jeb had swung his guitar around, strummed a chord, and a burst of energy from the tune blew off the man's helmet.

The guard stumbled backward, shielding his now exposed face.

"Run," Jeb mumbled, taking a few blind steps backward. "I said—RUN!" He raised his arm high in the air and brought it down on the strings. Another chord rang and a different blast came from the guitar.

Theo hesitated as he watched the armored man forced to the ground by magical, floating runes.

Jeb strummed one last time before turning to run.

Theo caught a glimpse of the guard being engulfed by the bits of grass in the dirt.

Jeb grabbed his arm, yanking him up the road. Theo took one last glance over his shoulder as they crossed the treeline. The armored man was no longer to be seen and a new set of riders were galloping their way into the city.

He wanted to see the castle—his home—but right as he tried to stop, his collar was yanked and he was pulled from his feet.

THE WAILING FOREST

Theo tried his hardest to keep up with the other two as they made their way deeper into the dense trees that surrounded the valley where the castle sat. Up close, the trees were much bigger than he had imagined from his balcony in the castle.

The sharp bramble patches scraped and stabbed through Theo's tattered and bloody clothes as he broke the forest border. The salty stench of his own sweat combined with the heavy aroma of dried ale made him nauseous.

As the rising sunlight vanished behind the canopy of the forest, the darkness surrounded him and he could barely see in front of him. He tried to keep his eyes on Jeb and Nila but he had to watch his every step. His exhausted body cried for rest as he pushed on through the maze of trees. Every step was a bigger battle than the last.

Jeb and Nila moved unfazed by the forest with Oli draped over Nila's shoulders. Jeb was climbing over fallen trees like they weren't massive obstacles. He would vault himself over or duck underneath the low-hanging branches. Nothing seemed to slow him down in a world much larger than he was.

Nila glided across the uneven ground. Each step was calculated and swift. No more than the faintest sounds of rustling leaves could be heard when she moved.

But they were too quick for the weary prince and eventually, he lost sight of them.

"Hello?" Theo sheepishly called out into the trees, nervous he would alert wandering predators.

There was no answer.

"Jeb? Nila?" He tried again. "Oli? Anyone?"

Total silence.

Theo grew anxious. He had never been so far from his home. He had never left the kingdom's borders before, and he had never left the castle unattended in his life.

"Maybe the king was right," he mumbled to himself. It stung his ears to hear him say it out loud. "There is a lot more to this world than I thought. I'm way over my head here and it's going to cost me."

In a huff of defeat, Theo sat down on the forest floor, his back against a fallen tree trunk, and he stared off hopelessly into the canopy.

For a brief moment, a ray of sun broke through. It didn't offer any warmth or very much light as it vanished just as quickly as it appeared.

Theo knew he was alone.

"I don't blame you," Theo mumbled to the empty forest, "I just wish you were here to save me." He slid back against the trunk trying to find a comfortable position to rest his body.

There was little resistance as he slipped into his dreams. None of them made sense but each one had the same hopeless feeling as the last. His mind raced while his body remained motionless.

He dreamt of his mother and sister, the monster he once called father and king, and the long wait at the Tankard Knight all filled his head. Many different faces and places melded together into one long tale that didn't seem to come to an end.

But before he could have a coherent dream, Theo was jolted awake by a sudden shriek. He threw himself forward, sitting up and away from the tree trunk. His heart pounded in his chest and between his ears as cold sweat poured down his forehead.

Another horrifying shriek echoed through the forest and Theo's blood froze. Instinctually, he sprang to his feet and scanned his surroundings, but there was nothing there. The forest was exactly how he remembered it.

He shook his head, trying to reset himself. "Jeb?" he called out into the empty forest, "Nila? Oli?"

Again, there was no answer.

"Alice?" he mumbled softly. He knew she wouldn't be there but something inside him hoped and prayed she was. "Alice? Is that you?"

There was an uneasy silence followed by another blood-curdling scream that echoed through the forest.

Before he could even think, his numb legs burst into a sprint, carrying him over and through the fallen foliage, paying no mind to the thorns now tearing the fabric of his pants and snagging his cloak.

The screams followed him as he charged around the dark obstacles. He never looked back. Whatever it was, it didn't sound friendly.

His boot caught an exposed root and he slammed face down in the dry soil. The pommel of his dagger jammed into his side and he could feel the blade slice across the side of his thigh. He shouted in pain and when the echo of his own scream faded, the forest was silent again.

Theo rolled onto his back, carefully maneuvering himself without cutting deeper into his leg, and he hesitantly pulled the dagger from his belt. Gritting his teeth, he applied pressure against his bleeding wound. He struggled with one hand to rip a strip off his cloak, managing to get the scrap of cloth secured around his leg, and he tied it tightly into a tourniquet.

Cautiously, he pulled himself back to his feet. He tried to put pressure on his injured leg and instantly pulled back onto the other.

"That's not good," he grunted as he righted himself against a tree.

It was difficult but Theo managed to hobble enough from tree to tree. The screaming had stopped but Theo wasn't convinced it was over.

A loud crunch caused Theo to freeze in his tracks. Clanking armor followed and before he could turn, a gloved hand snagged his arm.

"Your Highness!" A gruff voice came from behind a helmet.

Theo tried to jerk away but their grip was too strong.

"Your Highness, I'm with His Majesty's guard. You have nothing to fear," the helmet announced.

Theo, still trying to escape the guard's grip, looked the suit of armor up and down. It was the rider from before. He could see the dent in the lower jaw of the helmet where Jeb's blast struck the metal and large pockets of grass-filled soil poked between the plates.

"I'm here to take you home—"

The rider was cut off by a scream that made the hair on Theo's neck stand on end.

A shadow slammed into the rider, tackling them onto the hard ground, and fought viciously against the guard. The two figures rolled around in the dirt grunting and snarling with every strike.

Flipping from beneath the shadow that tackled him, the guard pinned the figure and raised the biggest stone he could find high above his head.

A high-pitched whistle sang through the air and the ring of metal being pierced filled the moment. Theo stared in fright at the guard who was frozen with the stone still raised and a large spear-like arrow now protruding from both sides of his torso.

The guard collapsed to his side, dropping the stone as he hit the ground, lifeless.

The shadowy figure quickly got to their feet and started lifting the guard's body over their shoulders. They stood up and Theo finally got a sight of how tall this being was.

Another larger, heavier hand wrapped around Theo's shoulder.

He leaped in fear and spun around. A large, muscular being with skin that faded from green to yellow and was painted with red markings towered over the prince.

A deep, rumbling voice came from the large being. It was in a language Theo had never heard. He could see that the being was waiting for a response but Theo was so panicked that he just stared back, paralyzed with fear.

The being's shoulders deflated. They grunted out something else before waving their massive hand in front of Theo's face.

There was no resistance as Theo blacked out. His eyes hadn't fully shut as the larger being bent down and hoisted him off his feet. As his vision faded to black, he felt the bouncing of being carried over their shoulder.

Thoughts flashed in the darkness. Images of Oli, memories of his mother, and visions of him with someone he's never seen.

Theo let out a small grunt as he snorted himself awake.

He blinked his eyes open and the forest was gone. He stared up at the walls made of stretched, tanned canvas that surrounded him and met in a cone towards a small opening in the top. There was a small column of smoke, gray and puffy, floating through the opening.

Cautious of his wounded leg, he attempted to sit up.

He was laying in a cot made of a canvas similar to the walls, and layered with furs.

Rolling onto his left shoulder, he noticed that his leg didn't hurt. In fact, nothing hurt anymore.

The prince quickly sat up in his cot, swinging his legs over the side and placing them on the ground. There was a pelt laying on the ground and he felt the fur between his bare toes. It was soft and was like nothing he'd ever felt beneath his feet. There was no rug, carpet, or blanket in the castle that compared.

Warmth spread across the floor from the small fire burning in the corner away from the canvas walls. His eyes adjusted to the flickering, low light as he noticed there was another cot on the other side of the tent.

It was unoccupied at the moment but he could see that it had been disturbed recently. He stood up from his cot, slowly putting his weight on his leg. Without any pain, he walked around the fire. His joints were stiff and there was a bit of popping but he was happy to be moving.

The canvas walls rustled from the other side. Theo scrambled for something to defend himself with and he grabbed his mother's saber that was beneath his cot. Drawing the blade, he pointed it towards the noise.

One of the panels in the canvas walls split open and a figure ducked through.

Theo was blinded by the light flooding through the opening as the figure stood up inside and the tent closed. His vision returned and Theo saw Oli holding a bundle of wood in his arms.

"Theo!" Oli burst out with a smile, dropping the wood and ignoring the blade pointed at him.

"Oli?" Theo deflated with excited relief. He dropped the saber to the ground and embraced his friend.

Oli was taken back as Theo wrapped his arms around his shoulders.

"Your Highness—"

"No," Theo cut him off as he pulled back, "you never have to call me that ever again. You are my closest—my greatest friend and I am happy that you are alive!"

"I'm glad you're alive too," Oli tilted his head with confused delight.

"What happened to us?" Theo finally asked, kneeling down for the saber. He turned back to his cot, sheathed the saber, and sat on the edge of the frame.

Oli's jaw tightened and his face wiggled with indecision.

"Are we back home?" Theo continued to question, "did we get intercepted by the guard?"

Oli pulled a couple of sticks from his pile on the ground, placed them on the fire, and then tucked the rest against the base of the tent. He sauntered over to the other cot and stared down at it.

Theo could see the contemplation of him deciding to sit or stand. The pointed tips of Oli's ears twitched for a second as he continued to gaze at the suspended bedding.

"Something *has* happened to us," Oli spoke soberly.

The words sat in Theo's ears. He knew the truth but didn't want to believe it.

"We're not far from home," Oli choked out, "there's a guard's post to the west. However—" his words caught in the back of his throat, "I don't think we'll be able to go back."

Theo watched his friend nervously avoid eye contact. The tension was heavy in the tent and neither of them knew how to break it.

"We've been here for a couple of days now," Oli sighed. Theo adjusted and tilted his head with confusion. Oli caught the gesture and turned to face the prince, "what do you remember last?"

Theo averted his eyes to the ground and tried to recall. "I—no, *we*—were attacked and chased from the castle. My sister saved us. We escaped with her handmaiden..." A knot formed in his throat as he remembered Ashti's fate. "She—ahem—she escorted us to the city where we met two people and left the kingdom."

Theo scrunched his nose, closed his eyes, and furrowed his brow as he tried to remember more.

"We got separated in the forest and I was attacked—or I was saved?" Theo mumbled as he pieced together the blurs. "Someone picked me up and ran away with me. That was when everything faded into dreams."

Oli's ears stopped twitching and Theo saw his shoulders roll forward to hide his body language.

"Oli," Theo stood from his cot, "where are we?"

WAKING UP

Oli opened his mouth to speak, but before he could explain, the tent opened again and a small figure wandered in followed by a much taller figure.

The canvas closed behind them and the fire illuminated the figures revealing Jeb and Nila.

"Well, I'll be," the halfling smiled, folding his arms across his chest, "you're quite a resilient one. The witches said it was going to be a week or more before you would come through."

Theo stared blankly back at him.

"Right," Jeb frowned. He turned to Nila and pointed at Theo, "do you think this is another one of those sleepwalking things again?"

"I'm awake," Theo said.

"Oh thank the gods," Jeb sighed with relief, "I wasn't sure you would stay down after the last—"

"Where am I?" Theo asked abruptly.

Jeb froze with his eyes locked on the prince.

"Theo," Oli interjected as he moved around the fire.

The prince jolted to his feet, drew his saber, and pointed it at Oli again. "Not another step," he warned, "I've asked three times now and nobody wants to give an answer. This is the last time I will ask patiently. This tent is not one of the king's. Have I been unconscious for days? And what's this I'm hearing about witches and sleepwalking?"

Jeb gave an innocent shrug.

"You were supposed to explain to him when he woke up," Nila scolded Oli.

"I didn't have a chance," Oli defended himself, "you two walked in before I was able to."

Theo kept the saber trained towards Oli, "I'm giving you time now. Speak!"

Oli looked to the others, closed his eyes, and let out a heavy sigh. "We're in a camp outside the empire's borders."

Theo didn't wince. His eyes locked on Oli's.

"Our escape was meant for your sister," Oli continued, "she planned the whole thing."

Theo's stern expression cracked as the corners of his mouth twitched.

"Your sister was going to flee the kingdom," Oli swallowed. He looked deep into the prince's eyes as his words hung in the air.

Theo lowered the blade between them.

"We weren't supposed to be chased into the forest," Jeb spoke up, "and neither of us noticed you fell behind. When we did, we had already come too far for us not to come back for you, we had no choice."

"So that was you who pulled me from the forest?" Theo glared at Jeb. "Someone—two of them—murdered a guard and I blacked out."

"*That*," Nila clipped, "was your generous host."

"We came across them in the Wailing Forest trying to find you," Jeb jumped in to release the tension Nila was creating. "They went off to find you while we escaped to camp."

"Who was it?" Theo mumbled.

The tent's door flapped open once again and Theo didn't recognize the figure as they stepped into the fire's light.

They stood next to Nila, not quite as tall but still a large presence in the now crowded tent. Greenish-yellow skin peeked from beneath a beaded tunic and woven shawl across their shoulders. Their lower jaw came to a point at their chin and two tusks poked from behind both sides of their lower lip. Thick, long, braids of dark hair draped down the back of their neck and rested on the front of their chest.

Theo started to swing his blade out between him and the newcomer but Oli lunged over the fire, grabbing the blade of the saber, and placed himself between the two.

Knocking the prince back into the cot, Oli bowed his head towards the new member. "This is Theo, Alice's brother."

The prince pulled himself back up, grabbing his friend's arm, and yanked himself out of the cot. Stumbling as he found his feet, Theo presented himself aggressively towards the being.

"Your Highness!" Oli snapped as he grabbed the prince's arm.

Theo felt something warm and wet soak his sleeve beneath Oli's palm.

"Theo," Jeb straightened his posture, "this is Rhan, Chief Daughter of the Woya tribe."

Every muscle in Theo's body tensed. He'd heard that word before and it left a bad taste in his mouth. He could hear his father's voice, angry and echoing down a hallway. It was the king screaming the word with malice. Swearing and cursing the Woya. Blaring his desire to rid them from the world along with the other vermin.

It filled Theo with rage and he was starting to shake with anger. Then he felt the still-warm liquid on his arm trickling down his wrists and dripping off his fingers.

He broke his glare with the woman and looked at the puddle of red on the floor next to his bare foot. Oli released the prince and he saw the deep gash in Oli's palm.

"It is an honor to meet you, Your Highness," Rhan bowed her head. "My father will be pleased to find out you're awake. I will let you all be. I'm sure he is eager to meet you." She turned to exit and looked at Nila, "I will leave the water and rags outside if you should need them. When the prince is ready, bring him to see my father. He'll be anticipating him."

She turned back to Theo with a smile, gave him one last nod, and went out of the tent. Theo noticed three white and brown feathers tucked in her hair where the braids met the back of her head.

As the tent closed behind Rhan, all eyes turned onto Theo.

"Alright, sit the hell down and let us talk," Oli clipped as he adjusted himself and started tending to his hand.

Theo, filled with red-hot embarrassment, returned his mother's saber to its sheath and sat down on the cot.

Oli pulled a pack from beneath the other cot and yanked out a bundle of yellowish-white cloth. He wrapped it around his bloody hand, tying the two ends of the bandage over his knuckles, and then he sat mirrored to Theo. Jeb wandered over to the cot and took the spot next to Oli.

Nila moved her way to the open floor between the cots and the door. Putting her ankles together, she lowered herself to the floor and sat with her legs crossed.

"A lot is happening around you right now, kid," Jeb grunted. He cleared his throat and then held his hands out like he was playing his guitar, but there wasn't anything there. "You need to stay calm and keep an open mind as we explain everything. There are going to be parts that might strike an emotion but you need to understand the severity of the dangers that have arrived." Jeb continued miming a guitar and soft music started to fill the tent.

Theo shook his head, thinking he was imagining the sounds but he was really hearing it.

"This entire escape from the castle was not meant for you," Nila picked up, "none of this was supposed to be happening with you."

Theo shifted uncomfortably.

"Ashti, your sister's handmaiden, was instrumental in the communications to and from the castle. Everything she smuggled from the castle gave us a precise extraction plan for Alice," Nila continued. "For months, your sister plotted and planned. Provided us infiltration notes, rendezvous points, and contact phrases. Your sister's message that Oli gave us was a distress signal. She's in danger and couldn't escape."

"There's no way she's in danger," Theo argued, "she's back in the castle. Why would she be in danger—"

"Your father is a monster!" Oli burst out.

Theo's body froze.

Nila let out a small sigh, "Your father, as you're well aware—" she tapped the bridge of her own nose, "is an abusive, vile bastard."

"But there's more to this than your father's abuse," Jeb pushed the story forward.

Nila glared at him and nodded. "Yes, besides the domestic travesties, your father is a relentless tyrant on a multi-generational, genocidal, warpath outside of your precious kingdom."

The words slammed into Theo like bricks being hurled at him but he remained unaffected on the surface as he was trained.

"Long before you were born and still to this day, your father has plundered his enemies and allies alike. For the last fifty years, he's laid waste to many lands and homes. His armies

storm entire villages and tear families apart. Conquering innocent people's lives and brutally assimilating them into his
empire." Nila closed her eyes and drew a deep breath.

"After your father occupies and claims territories, his
soldiers begin shipping people away," Jeb carried on. "At first
they claim that certain beings are causing a disturbance. That
they must be relocated to the capital where they can be rehabili-
tated to the new society. But those people never come back and
after a while, more of them begin to vanish."

Theo could feel his chest twisting.

"You don't notice it when it's not your people," Nila said
under her breath, "you can try to keep your head down and look
the other way but it doesn't stop them."

"When the occupations start, the entire community is
warped," Jeb swallowed hard, "and that's understating it. The
communities are devastated by what the soldiers call a
Cleansing."

"Theo, your father is trying to wipe the world clean of all
other races," Oli spoke, his voice calm but shaken.

Theo looked at Oli with a confused expression.

"Your father is committing multiple levels of genocide in an
attempt to remake the world in his image," Oli elaborated.

Theo shook his head, "What do you mean by other races?"

"Theo," Nila interrupted, "he means us. Elves—" she
gestured to herself and Oli, "halflings—" she pointed at Jeb,
"there are dwarves, gnomes, infernals, and so many others I've
never met myself. This world is filled with beings of all sorts and
your father wants to end that."

Theo blinked at her, stunned by the influx of information

"Have you ever met anyone like us?" Nila asked, taken back
by his glazed reaction.

Theo shook his head.

All three of them stiffened.

"The king never had guests outside of his closest advisors," Theo explained. "Beyond the few dignitaries from his allies in the west, I was unaware the world was so diverse. That's how my father—" the words were trapped in the back of his throat, "that's how the king raised me."

The air grew tense inside the tent.

"He told me that I would always be superior. That because of my blood, I was rightfully above the rest of the world." His heart began to pound in his chest. "He taught me to destroy those who would tell me otherwise."

The empty stare of realization was painted all over Theo's face. He pieced together all the teachings his father ever gave him. The talks about treating lesser beings like animals. Degrading anyone within his presence including his own children. The way he spoke to his queen. All of these memories suddenly flooded Theo's mind and made him sick to his stomach.

"Your sister wanted to leave that all behind. She wanted nothing more than to be free from your father's treachery," Nila spoke through gritted teeth. "She was going to liberate your father's labor camps. There were plans to siege your father's castle until he surrendered his crown. Alice has a vision for this world but now that she's trapped beneath your father's fist, her visions will die with her."

"That's why your sister was escaping, to meet with her allies and contacts. Phase One she called it," Jeb said. "It's what *we* were hired for." He continued to strum the air and music played softly underneath the crackling fire.

Theo took a deep breath as he tried to swallow everything. He hesitated for a moment but then he looked at Nila and asked, "What are the Woya?"

Nila looked back at the prince surprised. "They're a tribe of native nomads. They've wandered the plains that border the

Wailing Forest for hundreds of generations. Long before your father's empire began threatening their existence."

"But *what* are they?" Theo clarified.

"Orcs," Oli clipped. "Native Orcs."

Theo wanted to ask what an Orc was, but he was sure he understood. "Rhan?"

The three nodded.

"The beings who pulled me from the forest?"

Again, they nodded.

"And the chief?"

"Biggest one of them all," Jeb smiled. The tune of the invisible guitar shifted but remained soft.

Theo placed his hands on his knees and stood from his cot. He drew in a long, deep breath and let it out slowly through his nose. "I was never the diplomat," he mumbled, "that was always my mother's expertise." He looked at Oli who was avoiding his gaze. He looked over at Jeb who was now focused on the disembodied music coming from his hands. Finally, he locked eyes with Nila, "The chief is waiting for me then?"

"You're sure you're ready to go?" Oli furrowed his brow. The tips of his ears curled slightly before releasing back to their resting position. "There's a lot more we need to prepare you for."

Theo brushed himself off, strapped his belt around his waist with the saber secured tightly to his hip, and looked at the others. "I've spent my whole life preparing to meet and represent the king's crown." He reached under his cot and pulled the muddy boots out, "should this be our demise, it has been an honor knowing you all—"

"What do you think is about to happen?" Jeb squinted at Theo.

"I don't know what's going to happen," Theo shrugged as he pulled the first boot over his foot, "I'm hoping that they don't decide to take us prisoner and eat us." He yanked the second boot on and laced them.

"If you say something like that, they might kill you," Nila shook her head. "Where in the world did you get that nonsense?"

"Children's ghost stories meant to try and scare them into behaving," Oli chimed in. "War stories of prisoners being forced to watch their fallen be feasted upon by monsters before they managed to escape."

"I did watch one of them slaughter an innocent guard in the forest," Theo added, "they obviously have little restraint in battle."

"You were stranded on a stealth mission because you were not only unaware of the protocol but you also had to process massive amounts of trauma within a small period of time with little to no rest or break," Jeb blurted out. His tone was playful but direct and sharp. "If they had let that guard go, what do you think might be the first thing he'd have done after we fled?" The music stopped as he pulled his fingers from their invisible instrument and he rested his elbows where the body of the guitar would be.

Theo hesitated to react. He waited for Jeb's elbows to twitch from not being supported but the man didn't move.

"I—"

"You didn't think that far," Jeb clipped, "because you had no idea what was happening. We let the guard go free and they return to your father, bends his ear about how you were abducted by the natives—"

"Who they all believe are cannibals apparently," Nila interrupted.

"That too," Jeb agreed, "so now what does your old man do? Gathers a cause among his soldiers to attack and invade the native lands. I know this ale is hard to swallow but your father isn't too keen on leaving survivors."

Theo stood frozen.

"Everything you think you know about these people—" Jeb pinched the air between both of his index fingers and thumbs. He pulled his hands away from each other like he was presenting a string. Then he pantomimed crumpling the string between his hands. "Forget all of it," he finished, tossing the pretend ball of string over his shoulder.

Theo could feel Nila's glare peering into him from his right. He resisted looking over at her for a long while but his eyes decided to twitch and they locked eyes. A chill shocked Theo's spine.

"When you greet the chief," Nila spoke intensely, not breaking her gaze as she rose from the floor, "you will show nothing but the utmost respect you're capable of presenting. When we reach his tent, you will remove your saber and boots outside. It's a sign of respect to the home and a gesture of trust towards your host."

Jeb hopped down from the cot and moved slowly towards the tent's door.

"The rest of us will not be there during your meeting," Nila continued, "it's just you and the chief. He will introduce himself first and you will let him. When he is done, you will bow your head, introduce yourself humbly, and when he tells you to... you will sit."

Nila stood tall, spun on her heels, and burst from the tent, nearly knocking Jeb over as he tuned his invisible guitar.

Jeb straightened himself, brushed off his chest, and smiled at Theo. "You're going to be safe. Trust the chief and he will open his home to you." He swung the missing guitar over his shoulder and across his back before making his way out of the door.

The tent went silent as the two boys remained. Oli tried to

ignore the tension by changing his shirt and removing his blade from his hip.

Theo watched, trying not to make eye contact. He wanted to speak to him, but nothing would come out.

"It's a lot to take in, isn't it?" Oli mumbled. "Everything you were raised to believe—the training and education they put us through to believe—I guess that was the key. *Believe*," he let the word roll from his lips. "It was all lies."

Theo felt the hairs on his arms stand on end.

"He bred us to be killers in his genocide parade across the world." The words hung in the air. "Those stupid stories. Telling us that we were above them. They were supposed to be the enemy and yet here I am among them, unharmed."

Theo didn't look away as Oli's eyes locked with his.

"These past few days have been quite a journey and I'm sure you're about to face more as the next couple of nights come and go. Jeb touched on you processing the traumatic hours leading up to your last memories and I'm not sure if that will help or hinder what's going on, but as your friend, I want you to know that I am at your side till the absolute end."

Theo stared at his companion as a warm feeling filled his chest. Oli's bottom lip quivered and his ears twitched. He adjusted his posture to try and hide the emotions building behind the stoic facade.

"Don't hide behind your pride," Theo comforted him, "if there's something you want to say, speak plainly with me."

"No," Oli shook his head. He wiped away the wall of tears that formed over his eyes, "you've got more pressing matters to deal with. Another time perhaps?"

Theo drew in a deep breath and let it out with a slow sigh. He smiled at Oli with a nod, and walked towards the door.

TA'GODA

Theo ducked through the opening of the tent and the bright sunlight blinded him. He heard voices and the sounds of children playing and when his vision came back, the noises faded. He saw dozens of orcs silently staring at him. They resembled the chief's daughter and the being from the forest.

Green and yellow skin, tusks poking from the lower jaw, beaded clothes, and some bared tattoos on various patches of exposed skin.

Theo moved between the tents, avoiding eye contact with the woman who stepped in front of a group of children protectively. He scanned the outskirts of the encampment looking for the chief's tent.

"Where are you going?" Oli called to him as he came out of the tent.

"The chief's—"

Oli pointed his thumb over his shoulder at the large tent set up on a ridge behind him in the middle of the sea of canvas.

Without a word, Theo corrected his direction and marched towards the center of camp.

Unlike the other, cone-shaped tents that pointed to the sky, the chief's tent was a dome with a proper curtain door.

The two boys stood nervously before the entrance.

"Promise me—"

"Nothing is going to happen. I'll be right here when you come out." Oli could see the anxiety on Theo's face. He reached out, placing his hand on the prince's shoulder, and gave him a tight squeeze.

Theo was hoping for words of encouragement or assurance but he understood and appreciated the gesture. He stepped towards the door, took a deep breath, and pushed his way past the curtain.

An aroma of herbs and perfumes choked Theo as he inhaled the hazy air. His eyes watered through the fit of coughing and a couple of seconds later he managed to fill his lungs with the thick air.

The interior of the tent was domed like the exterior. Woven rugs laid across the dirt floor and animal pelts hung over wooden benches that lined the walls.

Standing on the other side of the tent was a massive green being with a broad build and defined muscles. They turned and Theo recognized them instantly.

It was the orc who had carried him from the forest. Cuts and scars marred their chest. Black and red tattoos wrapped around both their biceps and a black bear claw was branded on the left chest. Their hair was parted down the middle and braided into thick, black, tails that rested in front of their shoulders like Rhan's.

Before anyone spoke, Theo collapsed to his knees and bowed his head at the being's feet.

"My name is Theodore, son to King George and heir to his throne. I come before you, a humble refugee from my own home, begging for your mercy," Theo proclaimed with his face on the floor.

The tent fell silent and Theo raised his head to see what had happened.

Standing behind the large orc was another, slightly shorter orc that Theo recognized was Rhan.

Her deep brown eyes locked with his as she tried to mask her excited smile. But the rosy color to her mossy cheeks gave her away.

Embarrassed, Theo slowly got back to his feet keeping his head bowed.

The larger being nodded towards the door and Rhan left swiftly.

As the curtain billowed behind her, the larger orc turned and fully faced the prince, towering over him from across the tent.

"Theodore, son of the Lady Maria," the orc bellowed, "raise your chin and look me in the eye as an equal."

Theo was frozen with shock at the mention of his mother's name. His chest twisted as he realized how long it had been since he'd heard her name.

"I am Chief Ta'goda, leader of the Woya tribe," the orc introduced himself. "You are accepted by my tribe. We will aid you in your time of need."

Chief Ta'goda picked up a piece of cloth off a bench and wiped the sweat from his forehead.

"Your sister—" the chief continued, his voice softer and more welcoming but with a heavy tone, "she is a brave young woman. Her sacrifices will not be forgotten by my people and will help shape the future of both our communities."

The chief looked Theo over and then gestured towards the fire burning in the corner of the tent. Folded woven rugs surrounded the pit and the chief sat down on one.

Hesitantly, Theo followed suit and sat with the chief.

"How do you know my sister?" Theo asked nervously as he lowered himself in front of the fire.

"Your family and my tribe—" the chief began as he folded his legs beneath him, "our history is long. Running deep like the ancient trees of the southern swamps. I've spent years communicating with your sister, and your mother before her passing."

Again, the mention of his mother struck Theo in the chest. Like a hand reaching into his body and squeezing his heart.

"Your sister—she wishes to liberate your kingdom. To remove your father from his throne."

"She—"

The chief nodded slowly, "She's seen the devastation and has felt your father's wrath."

"What was she thinking?" Theo burst out.

"Your sister has been preparing this for many years," the chief continued, "but now you sit before me in her place. A young boy, running from his home."

"I'm not running from my home," Theo frowned.

The chief nodded, "but you have been expelled from your home, no?"

Theo didn't like the question but he couldn't argue. He knew it was true.

"While you are in my care, we will protect you," Chief Ta'goda moved on, "I have sent a message to my nephew on the eastern plains. He will be anticipating your arrival in the next few days. His people will have everything prepared for the next leg of your journey."

Theo frowned again at the chief.

"He will be able to explain more once you are in his care," the chief answered.

"You too?" Theo groaned. He quickly snapped to attention, the blood rushing into his cheeks with embarrassment again.

"My apologies, that was an unnecessary tone." He could feel the sweat on the back of his neck trickle into the collar of his shirt.

"No, please," the chief said calmly, "you may speak your mind with me. Here, you are my equal. If you have a grievance, speak it. Tell what your heart has to say."

Theo hesitated to respond. It felt like a trap. "My friends—" the words felt weird to his tongue, "have been quiet about what's been happening to me. I've got the pieces about my sister but after being in a coma for days and waking up in a camp outside my home, I've come to need more than just pieces of a story."

Chief Ta'goda stared at Theo in deep thought. Theo wasn't sure if anything he'd said actually made sense and started to worry he might have to repeat himself again.

"In life," the chief spoke softly as he exhaled, "we must face tests of our strengths. Physical, mental, and spiritual. My ancestors before us, our friends and family now, and your descendants long after we're both gone from this world will all have to face similar battles. We do not get to choose these tests and occasionally they are much harder than we could prepare for. Sometimes these tests will devastate even the most resilient of creatures." Ta'goda paused to let his words sink in while Theo silently listened.

"I have seen the most fierce of warriors, larger and stronger than myself, reduced to nothing but cries of fear in the wake of these tests. My own people, returning to the homes they defended, only to feel foreign to their own beds," he continued. "They tell stories of the things they had to do in the heat of battle. Burdens that they prayed never to bear. But those who come to me are seeking to heal and make their peace with themselves." He looked at Theo with a fatherly look, "healing takes time and is a delicate process with those you care for."

Theo frowned, "I am no warrior. I have never been in a battle let alone had to kill."

The chief shook his head and let out a soft sigh, "you do not have to kill to be a warrior." He looked into the fire that separated the two of them. Without a word, the bulky orc stiffened his back. Something in his eyes said he had an idea.

"In the forest when I found you, there was a rider from your father's guard, yes?"

Theo nodded slowly as he remembered the blur of events.

"The guard nearly killed one of my own," the chief recalled, "and with little choice, I had to make a difficult decision."

"You killed an innocent man," Theo mumbled.

"He may have been," Ta'goda nodded, "and if there had been another way, he would still be an innocent man."

"You could have taken him prisoner," Theo argued, careful not to raise his voice.

"Which means I will forever have to carry that burden," the chief answered. "To take another life is not an easy choice. But my burden isn't the reason for mentioning our shared experience."

Theo stared back at Ta'goda confused.

"While I was carrying you off to safety, our warrior recovered the body."

"What?" Theo burst out. He jumped up from his mat and stepped back from the orc chief. "You took the body? Why? You should have left it there for a search team to find! They would have notified the family. Now he's missing and there is no evidence to return to the family!"

Ta'goda waited patiently as the prince spouted off.

"It's true, isn't it?" Theo probed through a blur of emotions in his head.

The chief raised his chin curiously, anticipating Theo's harsh words. "Speak," the massive orc clipped.

"Did—you eat him?" Theo muttered with fear.

The chief's jaw went tight with frustration. He closed his

eyes and took a deep breath before carefully rising from the floor.

Theo eyed the large orc man as he wandered away from the fire. Tension floated through the thick, smoky air.

Ta'goda leaned over one of the benches and pulled a tanned leather tunic with beads laced on strands along the arms. He carefully pulled the tunic over his shoulders and pulled his thick black braids out of the collar to rest on his chest again. "I want to show you something," he said calmly as he picked up what looked like a crown of feathers from the same bench.

Carefully, the mountainous orc placed the feather bonnet on his head and when he turned back towards the prince it was an elegant headdress that covered the top of his head. Each feather was secured by rolls of fabric that were woven into the headband. Dangling on the sides and covering the chief's ears were more feathers with small tufts of fur.

"There are many more tests ahead of you, young Theodore," Ta'goda said, "and the world is a lot larger than the confines of your father's palace. Much of what you think you already know will quickly turn against you and in some cases, will cost you." He stepped around the prince and went over to a chest against the wall.

The wooden lid creaked as Ta'goda gently opened it with the tips of his fingers. He reached deep into the chest and Theo was filled with panic.

"Please, I didn't mean to offend—"

But before Theo could beg for his life, the chief turned to face him again, and resting along his forearm was a long, decorative pipe. Leather bands wrapped around the shaft and two brown, spotted feathers hung from the middle. The pipe was double the length of Ta'goda's forearm and he held it out toward Theo.

"Take this and hold on to it," the impassive orc demanded.

Without a nod of acknowledgment, Ta'goda placed it in Theo's hands and made his way out of the tent.

Theo stood there for a moment, trying to understand what was going on.

He delicately examined the pipe in his hand. It was hand-crafted and whittled with artistic care. He gently ran his thumb over the leather grip, sliding his hand upwards, and lightly felt the feathers between his fingers.

"Are you coming?" The calm chief's voice came from outside the tent.

Theo scurried after Ta'goda and ducked through the door.

The entire tribe was out and working communally. Children chased after each other with stacks of small tinder, bunches of dead leaves, and as much dry grass as their hands could hold. Elderly members sat in circles around large pots cooking together in packs. Parents with infants bundled against their chests handled stacks of feathers while others prepared a fire pit.

Doing his best not to fall behind the towering orc's brisk pace between the tents, Theo tried to watch a couple of boys not much older than himself prop wood together inside the stone surroundings of the fire pit.

But the chief didn't break his stride. He greeted people as they passed him and didn't miss a single hello. Theo could hear him ask how they were doing or how someone in their family's health was.

After a couple of minutes, Theo and Ta'goda stepped outside of the village of tents and onto a dirt trail that continued up the side of a small hill. Ta'goda led them out of sight of the camp. Theo clutched the pipe in his hands tightly, his anxiety growing as they pushed further into the rolling hills of dry grasses.

"You're going to be fine," Theo whispered to himself. "Keep an open mind—"

He caught a glimpse of the trail in front of Chief Ta'goda. Another orc with similar greenish-yellow skin, lower jaw tusks, and black hair braided down their back. Although they were smaller than Ta'goda, Theo straightened his back to maintain his own height.

Ta'goda quietly stopped and took a seat on a larger stone outcropping away from the younger orc. Theo stood and watched cautiously.

The orc stood motionless, staring over a pile of rocks. At the head of the pile was a wide bowl that held a low fire. They wore nothing more than pants that were made from the same tanned hide as Ta'goda's tunic. Dangling against his hip was a small bundle of feathers strung together with an assortment of beads and leather.

The prince stood in silence watching the scene. He didn't know when his place to speak was but also wanted to be assured that he wasn't in any danger.

"Your Highness—" Ta'goda said, patting a smooth portion of the boulder he sat on.

Theo gave him a nervous smile, nodded, and joined the chief. They sat quietly for another couple of minutes before Theo finally broke.

"What are we doing?" he whispered to the chief.

"Observing," Ta'goda grunted stoically, not taking his eyes off the standing orc.

Another couple of minutes passed and Theo started to grow restless.

"Your Highness," Chief Ta'goda spoke calmly, "I ask that you respect our traditions and observe patiently with me."

Theo's face went hot with embarrassment. He immediately straightened his posture and sat as still as he could.

More time passed and the sun started to dip behind the far-off horizon.

"Now, Theodore," Chief Ta'goda said again, "this is a Woyan ritual."

Theo silently nodded, trying to hide the evident confusion still on his face.

"Do you remember how I spoke of a person's trauma?" Ta'goda asked.

Theo bobbed his head.

"Something that is often overlooked is the trauma of battle," Ta'goda continued, "as a warrior, trained or not, you come to understand what your duty is on the battlefield. To lay down one's life in order to protect one's home and people is a task none could refuse. But to take another's life for that cause—" Ta'goda stopped.

Theo turned to look at the chief who was intently watching the younger orc. His posture presented him larger than before, and in the few remaining rays of light, the Chief Ta'goda had a heavenly glow surrounding him.

"To take another life is something that can destroy even the strongest from within," Ta'goda finished.

Theo glanced down and saw the chief's massive hands tightly gripping the tops of his knees. White knuckles protruding from his mossy-colored hands.

"Every warrior is trained for this decision," Ta'goda's words intensified their meaning but his inflection remained stoic, "to kill on the battlefield and value one life over the other. To throw your humanity aside and return a person to the earth. This is a terrible burden to hold on your mind but a heavier one on a person's soul."

Theo felt the blood rush out of his cheeks, leaving his face frozen with cold sweats.

"Should a warrior have to carry that burden, they must make their amends to the worlds beyond."

ANCESTOR'S DANCE

The last remaining rays of sunlight vanished behind the horizon and a choir of crickets chirped to life. A gentle breeze brushed over the three sitting on the hill, sweeping through the prince's hair like fingers combing his curls.

Sparks crackled from the fire within the bowl and the warrior began stomping their feet around the mound of stones in a powerful dance. As the warrior made their way towards the fire, Theo saw their face.

He was a young orc man, not much older than Theo's sister, with red markings painted across his hollow cheeks. He looked thin and exhausted as if he had been out here the entire time Theo was unconscious.

As the warrior passed the bowl, it burned brighter and hotter than before, and he threw his head up towards the sky. With a deep breath, he let out a falsetto cry and started singing to the moon and stars to the beat of his own feet.

The moment resonated inside Theo's chest. He felt connected to his surroundings and new emotions flooded his heart. Sorrow, pain, confusion, rage.

The warrior finished his fifth dance around the stones and came to a halt in front of the burning bowl. The flames went as high as his shoulders, and he stood only two steps from it.

Ta'goda rose from his seat, holding his hand up to stop Theo from following him, and he went to stand at the other end of the ritual from the warrior. He held his arms out towards the young orc and let out his own falsetto cry to the heavens.

The warrior's eyes were locked on the fire before him as he responded to the chief's song with his own. Back and forth they called out with each other, their voices filling the valley with echoes far off in the distance.

Ta'goda bowed his head as his part ended and he stepped back from the stones. Gesturing to Theo, the chief motioned for him to join them.

As Theo stood with the mighty orc, he watched the warrior grab the bowl and turn the flames over his head, extinguishing the light.

"What is he—" Theo started to exclaim but Ta'goda raised his hand without looking at the prince.

The charcoal in the bowl rolled off the warrior's shoulders and chest, covering him in black soot. Hot coals landed on the matted grass where he stood and little wisps of white smoke climbed his legs.

"This ritual has been a tradition of my people since long before the Tribal Divides," Ta'goda explained. "When one's life has been spared at the cost of another, we must give the body back to the nature around us and bless the soul's departure. This world provides us with our bodies and when our time has come, we must return our gifts and journey to the next world."

Theo stared at the warrior standing in the moonlight.

"This journey takes time and can be perilous for souls lost during battle," Ta'goda continued, "many spirits are stranded when they leave their bodies. Left wandering our world unprotected." He raised his hand and gestured at the warrior.

The young orc stood over the stones, his chest inflating and deflating as he breathed heavily. Sweat beaded on his brow and shoulders, leaving trails through the dark soot.

"He has been here for three days," Ta'goda said, "watching over the body until it is ready to return to the earth." He gestured up to the sky, "as the night sets, the gates between this world and the next are opened. When he is ready, he will call upon our ancestors as guides to the next world."

The warrior threw his head back again and stared at the sky. He opened his mouth and let one last song into the night.

Blue flames erupted from beneath the mound of stone and the red marking on the young orc's face illuminated. His eyes flashed over and began glowing pure white.

The flames grew larger and took on humanoid shapes around the stones. Heads and arms became more defined as faces formed noses and eyes. Men and women wearing many variations of the same outfit the warrior wore. They stood shoulder to shoulder and surrounded the grave ceremoniously.

Theo watched in awe. He had never seen such a ritual and for a moment he couldn't tell whether he was dreaming or not.

With their arms outstretched, the elemental beings and the warrior danced.

They followed the same circle from before, every stomp in time with the others. Voices gradually filled the air from a distance and grew louder as they got closer. Each individual voice added to the choir that filled the air.

A small yellow light formed in the center of the stone mound, rising from the grave and floating in the air above it.

Everyone came to a halt but continued to stamp in place with their arms outstretched towards the orb of light.

Another humanoid figure, smaller than the blue flames,

formed from the yellow light. More familiar features formed until Theo recognized the face of the rider from the morning of his escape. There was no sign of Jeb's attack or the arrow that took his life. He stood there in an ethereal form.

The blue flames spun in circles, their stamping growing more intense as the blues and yellows started to swirl together, becoming a column of light out of the grave. The vortex stretched and thinned until it touched the sky. A bolt of lightning lit up the night and the thunder shook the earth.

Waves of green, blue, and purple light rippled across the dark canvas above. Yellow light within the blue flames moved into the heavens and with another bolt of lightning, all the light vanished overhead.

There were no more blue flames or green waves in the sky. The warrior's eyes no longer illuminated his face and the red markings faded.

Theo looked up at the endless black sky anticipating stars, but there was nothing. Even the moonlight was gone. He took a deep breath and slowly exhaled to calm his nerves.

One by one, he watched the stars flicker back to life in the night sky like little dots poking through a black curtain.

Ta'goda let out a small grunt and straightened his posture. "The Ancestor's Dance is a sacred part of my people."

The chief moved across the quiet ritual site, stopped behind the catatonic young orc, and the warrior collapsed into Ta'goda's arms. Carefully, he lifted him off the ground and walked back the way they came. Ta'goda didn't say a word as he passed Theo.

The prince fell in line behind the prodigious orc and followed him back down the trail. His mind raced with questions he wanted to ask but he knew this wasn't the time.

Hiking back felt like it took forever as they quietly walked through the dark night. Theo noticed the moon had returned but that wasn't what caught his attention as they crested the next hill.

Firelight came from the center of the camp as it came into view. A stack of gray smoke plumed against the now deep purple and blue sky and masked many of the stars. Ta'goda pushed on down the trail.

Theo thought he could hear his heart racing in his chest but as they got closer, he realized it wasn't his heart at all. Those were the sounds of drums.

BOOM-bum-bum. **BOOM**-bum-bum.

Each strike filled Theo with energy. He rolled his shoulders back as a wave of confidence shot up his spine.

Ta'goda continued to lead through the tight alleys between the tents, towards the flickering light and beating drums.

They both stepped out from between the tents and into an open circle filled with people. Most of them were orcs like Ta'goda and the warrior, but there were a handful of others that Theo noticed.

Everyone was gathered around a roaring bonfire in the middle of the open area. An older orc man paced around the fire with a long stick that he would poke and prod the burning wood to keep the flames tall. Other beings dressed in feathers on their backs and heads danced around the man's fire.

A jingle came from the dancers as they pounded their feet in the dirt. Some of the feathered dancers held shields and fans of feathers while others shook large, decorated sticks that rattled from inside.

Ta'goda walked into the circle and everything came to a halt. The drums went silent, the dancers froze, and everyone looked to the chief who still carried the young man in his arms.

He approached the fire and carefully set the warrior at the feet of the Firekeeper.

The Firekeeper took his staff and raised it towards the sky.

He sang into the sky and started shaking his staff down towards the warrior. It rattled and the Firekeeper stamped his right foot in the dirt.

The entire crowd threw their heads back and joined the song.

Theo stayed in the back where Ta'goda left him. He was filled with more questions and had no idea what was going on. But something inside him loved this. Every second of what he was experiencing filled him with overwhelming joy. To be a part of a collective wasn't something he was familiar with.

As everyone shook their hands towards the warrior laying in the dirt, a single strike of a drum echoed, and everyone dropped to one knee with their heads bowed. Everyone but Theo and Ta'goda.

Completely caught off guard, Theo lowered himself to his knee and tried to hide the embarrassing red cheeks growing on his face.

Ta'goda lifted his chin high and turned in place. "My brothers and sisters—" Chief Ta'goda spoke to the crowd, his voice carrying through the entire valley, "visitors of my people —" he looked down to Theo, "we come together as one this evening. For tomorrow, we shall journey apart as we search for our next homes. As a tribe, as a people, and as children of Woyan kin, we celebrate tonight all those who are with us and those who have since gone to the next world. Let us give thanks to all those to come before us and give us this tradition. To the Ancestor Chiefs and to the Chiefs of our Tomorrow—" He held an arm out to the crowd.

From deep behind the packed ring of Woya standing outside the kneeling dancers, Rhan stood and walked to her father by the fire.

He wrapped his arm around her shoulders and they both hugged each other tightly.

"Take this evening to count everything that you hold dear. Laugh with those you hold close and make peace with those you don't. Thank the land for sheltering us and providing us with bountiful harvests. Praise the beasts of the prairie who gave us their bodies for warmth, tools, and meals. Rejoice in the Woya," Ta'goda preached. "Sing until the morning rooster calls to the ravens of the night to bring us the sun. Dance until your soul can no longer carry you." He released Rhan from under his arm and she stepped back into the ring of dancers and knelt with them.

Ta'goda took one step away from the fire, turned to the Firekeeper, and joined his daughter on his knee.

The Firekeeper took his staff and planted the end in the ground right above the warrior's head. He reached into his belt and produced a fan made from feathers wrapped at the base. Carefully flicking it over the warrior's body, he mumbled a chant.

Theo didn't understand what the chant said but he could tell it was a prayer by the way he recited the words.

The Firekeeper started at the warrior's head and slowly moved the fan down to his feet. The crowd remained silent. After the last flick of the feathers, the Firekeeper let out a different song than the one before.

The drums pounded again as the man sang. In the ring of dancers, some of the men started tapping their feet, and the jingling filled the empty space between drumbeats.

Gradually, the rest of the crowd began singing along with the Firekeeper. The song grew louder and the echoes sang a distant harmony over the valley.

Theo hesitated, but the urge to join was much stronger than he imagined. At first, he kept his voice down to not be noticed. The longer he sang, the more confident he became. Words he'd never spoken or even understood started flowing from his mind to his mouth and came out as the same song he was hearing.

He raised his head now and looked around the crowd. Different beings who lived their own lives. No one around him cared who he was. He wasn't a prince or the son of a tyrannical king. Nobody told him about the atrocities his family caused. He was, for once in his short life, hidden among people and he never wanted to leave that moment.

As everyone carried the song and the drums thundered in the background, the Firekeeper turned to the fire. He reached into a pouch hanging from his belt and pulled out a handful of sandy-gray dust. He threw the powdery substance into the fire and it erupted with colorful sparks. Greens, purples, reds, blues, and yellows floated into the air before vanishing from sight.

Without even a reaction to the explosion of colors bursting in his face, the Firekeeper took his bare arm and shoved it into the bottom of the fire. He reached deep into the tall stack of burning wood and pulled out a piece of hot coal with his bare hand. His arm was unscathed as it left the roaring fire.

He held the coal in front of his chest and crushed it in his palm. Black dust puffed from between his fingers and coated the sides of his hand. With his other hand, he forced his thumb into the closed fist. He turned, knelt down beside the warrior still laying at his feet, and with his thumb covered in black, he wiped the soot across the unconscious man's forehead.

The ring of dancers jumped to their feet, all of them jingling as they stomped, and they sang with every step.

Ta'goda and Rhan slowly rose and moved towards the warrior. The Firekeeper sang his song as he marked the chief and his daughter with soot on their foreheads.

They joined the Firekeeper's song while the ring of dancers started circling the fire again to the beat of the drums.

Theo tried to see what was happening near the fire through

the moving dancers. He watched Ta'goda and Rhan both stick their hands into the fire but they didn't bring out coals.

In the chief's palm was a small yellow flame. It didn't burn him and he showed no signs of pain. Rhan held a blue flame with both hands that was much larger than Ta'goda's.

The two took their flames and lowered them over the warrior's body.

Theo lost sight of the flames from behind the feet of the dancers but when their hands came back into his sight, they were helping the warrior sit up.

The young man carefully got to his feet and the entire tribe cheered. Everything erupted with excitement as the entire tribe stood and danced.

Theo was lost in the whirlwind. Being carried with the crowd, he was spun around, shoved, and tripped. His anxiety started to take over and his vision tightened into a pinpoint. He tried to focus on the outside of the sea of people, trying to escape. But instead, he was dragged closer to the center. When he broke free from the group, he landed right at Ta'goda's feet.

"Theodore," the chief nodded down at the prince.

Theo scrambled to his feet, dusting off his shirt. Rhan stifled a small chuckle which caused Theo to blush.

Ta'goda turned and revealed the young warrior behind him, "I would like you to finally meet, Ahote."

Theo stared at the man for a moment, trying to process what was happening, and then out of muscle memory, the prince bowed his head. "It's a pleasure to meet you," Theo greeted the young man.

"I'm glad to see you're alright," Ahote responded. He approached the prince and tried to grab his shoulder.

Theo quickly retreated from the warrior. He'd never been approached by anyone outside the castle and in his head he could hear his father once telling him to never let a commoner touch him.

Something else inside Theo started to shout over the king's instruction. A little voice in the back of his head. His conscience telling him to keep an open mind.

The prince rolled his shoulders back and returned his step. "I must thank you," Theo spoke, "if it weren't for your bravery, I would probably be back in the king's custody."

Ahote hesitated to respond. "I'm sorry it had to come with the loss of one of your own."

The words struck Theo square in the chest. Like being charged by a bull and not getting out of the way. He'd never thought of his father's guards as people. Their lives were never a worry in his mind.

"I—" Theo tried to find the best words but nothing came out.

"There will be plenty of time to get to know each other," Ta'goda interrupted, "for now, Ahote—" he looked at the warrior, "go find your family. You've left your dear wife alone with the children too long. I'm sure she will be very happy to see you again."

Ahote stood up straight and a smile broke across his face. "Thank you, Ta'goda," he bowed his head. He looked back at Theo and gave him a nod before taking off into the crowd.

"Your Highness," Ta'goda addressed Theo again.

The prince snapped to attention.

"Will you join us for tonight's feast?" he asked. There was a friendly tone to his question, breaking the stoic image he'd held since the two met.

FEAST OF THE HARVEST

Ta'goda and Rhan led Theo through the crowds of dancers and beings wandering the open space. They came to a small area in front of Ta'goda's tent where a woven blanket was set out with small rocks on the four corners to weigh it down. Ta'goda took a seat on the blanket while Rhan stepped into the tent. Theo stood for a moment, trying to decide who he should follow.

"Have a seat," Ta'goda offered, gesturing at the open space on the blanket.

The prince glanced around and noticed many of the people not in the dancing circle were setting up their own spots on the outer part of the open space. Families sat in circles around small children so they could roll and play. Other children, those old enough to walk and talk, chased each other through the camp.

He watched the dancers break into new dances as the drums changed their beats. Some of the members sang and their voices carried across the hills.

As Theo took his seat on the far corner of the blanket from Ta'goda, a young woman with pointed ears poking from beneath a mane of black curls approached the chief.

She had strings of colorful beads dangling from her left wrist all the way up to her shoulder. She pulled the first one off with her other hand and offered it to Ta'goda.

Without a word, the chief bowed his head and the woman placed the beads around his neck. She turned to Theo and offered him a string as well.

The prince nervously looked at Ta'goda who gave him nothing more than a small nod. Theo hesitantly bowed his head to the woman and felt her place the beads around his neck. She didn't say anything, only turned and continued down the line of people.

"Another sacred tradition of our people," Ta'goda explained, "when my ancestors first formed our elder tribes and began our nomadic life, they held a great feast. Orcs from different factions and families sat side by side to share meals and stories. Over the generations, it became a ceremony of thanks and peace among our tribes. Everyone has something to celebrate. As for our tribe, we spend the night giving our thanks to the earth for providing us our homes. We borrow from her soil to grow our crops. Maize and wheat grow tall and plentiful when the ground is fertile. The harvest marks our seasons of searching. To ensure the earth heals, we find new land to grow from. But on the final night, before we start our journey, we come together and feast!"

As he finished his thought, another woman approached the two of them. She was an older orc with salt and peppered hair pulled back in a long braid that coiled behind her head. In her hands, she held two long, green leaves folded in half.

She spoke to Ta'goda in a language Theo didn't know. Without a response, Ta'goda stood from his spot, gave the woman a tight hug with one arm, and took both leaves from her with the other hand.

She smiled, pulled the chief down to her level, and planted a kiss on his cheek.

"Thank you," Ta'goda smiled as she let him stand back up. "Ona Tara, le'hey yee."

The woman gave him a smile and went back into the crowd.

"Who was she?" Theo asked as Ta'goda handed him one of the leaves. The prince accepted the leaf and Ta'goda sat down again.

"We call her *Ona Tara* or the Feast Mother in your language," the chief explained as he scooped a handful of the leaf's contents into his mouth.

Theo looked down at his leaf and saw an assortment of food. Juicy, shredded, brown meat on a pile of corn kernels, beans, and rice. Resting beside the pile of grains and meat was a golden disk of fried bread.

He watched as Ta'goda tore his own bread and folded it between his fingers. He pinched a small bit of the meat with the bread and threw the whole bite in his mouth.

"She is the one in charge of the feast," Ta'goda continued through another mouthful of food. "Since the start of the harvest season, she has been collecting and preparing everything in front of you."

Theo took a small pinch of the meat and placed it on his tongue. He anticipated it to be stringy and chewy like the roasts he was accustomed to but the meat was tender and melted in his mouth. Flavors Theo had never tasted before danced across his tongue. Smoky tones preceded the sweet tang of berries and as the concoction of different flavors coated his tongue, something spicy kicked in and caught the prince off guard.

He choked out a cough as the tingling sensation took over. Burning filled his mouth and sweat formed on his brow.

"It will pass," Ta'goda assured him as he took another big bite. "That's the peppers you're tasting. They burn hotter than the flames of the ancestors and cleanse your body well."

Theo tried to inhale as much cool air as he could to subside the pain now resting on the sides of his tongue and lips.

"Drink some of this," Ta'goda said. He pointed behind the prince as another member of the crowd walked up offering him a wooden cup and Theo took it immediately.

He poured the contents into his mouth, hoping for relief.

It had a sweet flavor and stung against the portions of his tongue that still burned. A couple of seconds passed and the fire in his mouth faded.

"I—ahem—" Theo coughed as he cleared his throat, "I've never had—mhmm—those flavors before."

"My people take pride in their feasts," Ta'goda smiled.

"Mine don't," Theo said dryly. "The king has the means to feed the entire kingdom the most exquisite meals in the entire world but instead he hoards it all and boils it for himself."

Ta'goda gave a playfully uncomfortable look to the prince. "Boiling is meant to purify water and make stew. Why would you boil your food?"

"After trying this—" Theo smiled with another pinch of food from his leaf between his fingers, "I have no idea."

The two finished the contents of their leaves and watched as the dancers continued stamping around the fire to the beat of the drums.

Then a familiar voice called to Theo from among the crowd.

"Theo!" the voice rang in the prince's ear.

He scanned the camp until he saw Oli across the sea of people.

The young guard pushed his way past a group of children who ran the other way around him. He had five different strings of beads around his neck. Three of them had only red beads and the other two were a bright assortment like the ones around Ta'goda and Theo's necks.

Oli stopped before the blanket and bowed his head to Ta'goda.

"It's good to see you again, Olsdeyr," the chief greeted him. "He's quite a loyal friend, Prince Theo. You don't come by those very often."

Theo jumped up and pulled Oli into a tight hug.

"Thank you," Theo said as they let go of each other.

"What for, Your Highness?" Oli smirked.

"All of it!" Theo answered, not recognizing the sarcastic tone. "Being by my side through these past few days. Your entire life was uprooted because of me and you haven't looked back or abandoned me when there were ample opportunities—"

"Theo—" Oli tried to interrupt.

"You dragged me to my sister, fending off assassins, and continued to carry me to safety. You shared my first real drink with me—"

"Theo!" Oli clipped. "Shut up and let's enjoy the feast." He pulled a small pouch strung to his belt and opened it in front of the prince. The paper wrapping unraveled revealing two fluffy discs of bread stuffed with another type of meat and rice. He held the steaming food up and offered half to his friend.

Theo hesitated at first but smiled and accepted. The aromas of toasted spices and seasoned meat filled his nose. He took a cautious bite, wary from the burning flavors of the last meal.

It was pleasantly surprising like all the other experiences happening around him. Creamy and full of savory flavors that made him crave more.

Oli took a bite and Theo watched his eyes go wide.

"Oh, my—" Oli choked out through a second bite. "This is —wow."

"Like nothing you've ever had before, right?" Theo matched the excitement.

Oli nodded.

"Pace yourselves," Ta'goda chuckled as the boys stuffed the rest of the bread and meat into their mouths, "there is a lot more to enjoy as the evening goes on. Olsdeyr, come and join us."

"It would be an honor," Oli accepted.

The night continued with more food and drink brought around. The dancers broke apart while a single member stayed, and they went around the fire as the drums sped up. Losing his sense of time, Theo watched and enjoyed himself as the drums and the dancer slowed to another steady beat.

"I asked you to hold on to something for me, do you still have it?" Ta'goda asked Theo, interrupting his focus.

Theo panicked. He hadn't thought about the pipe since they were with Ahote. He quickly patted his chest and thighs hoping it would be there.

A quick scan of the ground around him and he saw the pipe was sitting behind him on the blanket.

Theo scrambled and fumbled as he plucked it off the ground before handing it to the chief.

"This is a sacred heirloom," Ta'goda smiled as he held the pipe in front of his chest, "it is passed down from chief to chief. I will one day give it to Rhan when she is ready to take my place just as my mother passed it on to me. It is a relic of our tribe. When my people first met your ancestors, Prince Theodore, they shared this pipe as a sign of peace." Ta'goda stood and walked towards the center of the camp. He stopped at the end of the blanket and looked over his shoulder. "It has been many generations since *our* people have come together. I wish to, as your people might call it, propose a toast."

The chief continued walking towards the fire. As he stepped into the dancer's ring, the lone dancer continued their steady movements. They reached behind their back and pulled out a flute made of animal bone. The dancer raised the flute to their lips and a beautiful whistle filled the air. They took long steps with flowing movements that changed with the notes.

From the circle of drums on the other side of the fire, one of the drummers began to sing with the flute's song.

Ta'goda walked with a grand stride through the middle of the feast. When he reached the fire all the music stopped and the tribe went silent once again.

"Na'yaway heiea untota," Ta'goda boomed over the crackling fire. "With the essence of the earth mother," he translated, "miaya nohe'ah sorwana, we become friends."

Ta'goda reached into a pouch on his hip and pulled out a pinch of something Theo couldn't see. The chief took his fingers from the pouch and stuck the contents into the end of the pipe.

The drums, flute, and singing began again as Ta'goda held the pipe above his head, and with one, quick, fluid motion, he put the pipe into the massive fire.

He pulled it from the fire seconds later, pressed the mouthpiece to his lips, and inhaled deeply. Ta'goda separated his lips and a gray ring of smoke floated from his mouth into the air above him.

He walked back towards the blanket and Theo grew nervous.

The music picked up and the energetic atmosphere of the feast returned. More dancers returned around the fire. The sound of jingling and stomping filled between the beats of the drums once again.

Ta'goda returned and offered the still smoking pipe to Theo. "My people have honored the tradition of sharing the gifts of the creator with our friends and allies. It is customary for the chief's guest of honor to take the second turn," Ta'goda explained.

Theo reached for the pipe cautiously, reminding himself to keep an open mind.

"I won't be offended if you should choose not to," Ta'goda

added, "I don't believe in forcing others to participate in our traditions if they are uncomfortable or unable to."

Theo's shoulders relaxed. "That's very respectable of you."

"I appreciate your kind words," Ta'goda smiled.

Theo returned the smile and accepted the pipe.

"Do not inhale too hard," the chief warned.

Theo nodded and put his lips to the mouthpiece. He tried to breathe in and immediately choked on the thick smoke that filled his lungs.

"Ack—" he gagged before bursting into a deep coughing fit. He could feel the sweat building on his brow and neck. His whole body heated up and his head started to spin.

Ta'goda carefully took the pipe from Theo and passed it behind him.

"Theo?" Oli called the prince.

Theo held up his index finger, still choking on the smoke.

"He will be okay," Ta'goda assured Oli.

"That—was not what I was—expecting," Theo choked through suppressed coughs as he regained control of his breathing.

Ta'goda burst with a peal of booming laughter and clapped Theo on the back with his massive hand.

The prince let out another cough and drew a sharp breath.

"I have one last tradition for you both this evening before I must return to my duties with my people," Ta'goda said.

MEDICINE WITCHES

The entire feast went dark as the massive bonfire suddenly extinguished. Theo's anxious instincts kicked in but he was confused when no one screamed or panicked in the dark.

Softly, the drums began to beat again and the rattling of the dancers added to the rhythm.

Boom-tat-tat-tat, **Boom**-tat-tat-tat, **Boom**-tat-tat-tat.

Breaking the darkness, six green flames started to burn in the bottom of the firepit. The small, individual fires didn't touch and barely came off the ground.

Behind Theo, Oli, and Ta'goda, the door to the chief's tent opened with a flourish. The three men saw six figures outlined by moonlight step out of the tent. They wore long masks that stretched high above the crown of their heads and black cloaks hid their shoulders.

The six figures stepped in time with the drums, slowly advancing towards the green flames. As they passed, another figure stepped out from the tent.

The being cupped a blue flame in their hands that illuminated their face. Theo and Oli both recognized Rhan.

She was wearing a new outfit. The three feathers that ran down the back of her neck were now displayed on top of her head. One feather pointed straight up while the other two pointed out to her left and right.

There were two colors painted on her face. A white, powdery substance masked the majority of her forehead and cheeks above her lips. Along her jawline was a line of red paint that went down to the base of her neck. She had a shawl draped over her shoulders and a long, beaded necklace that looped across her chest multiple times.

Without looking up from the flame in her hand, Rhan followed the march.

Theo watched in awe as the six lead figures dispersed evenly around the firepit. The six beings knelt down and put a hand beneath the individual green flames. Each of them slowly rose, now cradling a green fire in front of their chests.

Rhan joined the others around the firepit and she raised her flame high above her head.

Together, the seven held their fires over the charred stacks of wood and dropped them onto the pit. It erupted once more with a roar of light. A bonfire of flickering greens and blues lit up the crowd's faces. Above, the night sky filled with wisps of the same hues. Theo recognized this from Ahote's ritual earlier.

"Yoma'ta hey'ah ta," Rhan chanted towards the sky.

The six masked beings joined her chant, shaking their hands at the fire below.

Theo felt a warm sensation in his chest that reminded him of the healing potions his sister gave Oli as they fled the castle. He felt revitalized and full of energy.

Before he could make sense of this newfound feeling, Rhan was standing over him with her arms stretched out towards him. She waved her hands trying to get him to join her.

He tried to decline the invitation, but Oli was pulling him up while accepting the same offer from one of the masked beings.

Rhan took the prince's hands and spun him into the dancing ring. He caught his footing and tried not to trip over his own boots.

"Follow my lead," Rhan smirked at him.

The drums thundered and Theo felt their vibrations through the earth. It rocked him to the core and the revitalized energy from Rhan's chant turned electric in his chest.

Rhan and the masked beings broke into dance and before Theo could think about it, he followed her example. Together, Theo and Oli danced along with the chief's daughter.

"What's happening?" Theo asked as he looked down at his feet.

"You feel it, right?" Rhan smiled as she took his hands and started to spin.

"I've never done this before," Theo giggled like an excited child.

"But you have," Rhan said as she let him go dancing around the fire, "open your eyes and see for yourself."

Theo frowned. His eyes were open. He continued to dance, feeling the rhythm pulse through his chest.

With one last spin, Theo's vision was filled with blurs of blue. But they weren't from the fire or the sky, they were figures made of fire dancing with them.

Theo spun, laughed, and lost track of the dance.

After what felt like hours, the music stopped, and Rhan led the boys back to her father.

"Wow!" Oli burst with excitement. "What was that? Who were those people dancing with us?"

"That was a healing dance," Rhan smiled, "an ancient practice of Woya Medicine Witches."

"Witches?" Theo asked.

"Healers of our tribe who have abilities and utilize the natural remedies given to us by the creator," Rhan explained. "The six women behind the masks use their skills to cure our people of illnesses and curses."

"Why are they only women?" Oli leaned in eagerly.

"It's a power only women of our tribe are gifted," Rhan answered. "But even with that, only a few are born with these capabilities every generation."

"Are you one of them?" Oli squinted at her curiously.

Rhan nodded with a playful chuckle, "I am."

"You don't give yourself enough credit," Ta'goda said as he rose from his seat, "a chief and a healer. There has not been both in our lineage for over ten generations."

"It's not that big of a deal," Rhan shook her head bashfully.

"You will become a better chief than I ever could have been," Ta'goda proclaimed as he hung his arm over his daughter's shoulder. He gave her a tight squeeze, "you do our people proud, my child."

Rhan looked up at Ta'goda skeptically.

"I'm sorry," the chief straightened his posture, "I've had a few too many spirits. If everyone will excuse me for a moment." He bowed his head to the two boys and stepped away from his daughter. Without another look, Ta'goda walked around the side of his tent and vanished around the corner.

"Is he going to be okay?" Oli asked.

"He'll be fine," Rhan laughed, "it's rare that he gets to relax and enjoy himself like this. He has a very low tolerance of the wines."

Theo looked to Oli anticipating another question to come out, but instead, Oli was staring back at a group of young women who were looking his way and giggling to each other.

Theo leaned over and lightly punched Oli's shoulder. "You can go talk to them," he teased.

"What—no—Your Highness?" Oli stumbled over his words. His cheeks and the tips of his ears were bright red.

"Olsdeyr," Theo raised an eyebrow with a devious smirk, "as your *friend*, I demand you go over there and talk to them."

Oli shook his head, "No, I can't—I shouldn't."

"Even the chief is enjoying himself," Theo argued, "go, enjoy the feast."

Oli hesitantly stood and looked to the prince as if he were waiting for permission to walk.

"Would you go already?" Theo rolled his eyes jokingly.

A smile cracked across Oli's face. He turned and walked off towards the group of giggling girls.

"I should warn you," Rhan spoke up after Oli was out of earshot, "we're not going to see him for the rest of the night."

Theo looked at Rhan confused.

"Those are the Moh'ay sisters," Rhan explained, "they're the Ona Tara's granddaughters. He's going to be in a food coma before sunrise."

"I don't know," Theo smirked as he watched his friend turn back with a thumbs up, "he has quite the stomach. I once watched him devour a bowl of gray gruel and stale bread before being thrown into combat sparring. Back when he and I were just kids in school."

"Combat sparring?" Rhan's eyes lit up. "You're trained?"

Theo averted his eyes to the ground.

"Oh come on," Rhan pressured.

"We both were trained to be knights," Theo sighed, "it was something the king forced upon me. But for Oli, there was no other option."

"Do you remember any of it?" Rhan asked excitedly.

"Enough I could hold my own if I needed to," Theo shrugged.

"Come with me," Rhan demanded as she grabbed the prince's arm and pulled him towards the tents.

"What? Where are we going?" Theo frowned.

"I want to show you something," Rhan answered. She yanked Theo's arm again and his feet came loose.

The two ducked around the tents, making sure to not get caught by Ta'goda as they left the feast. With Rhan in the lead, they ran out of the camp and followed a trail to the tallest hill that overlooked the moonlit valley. On top of the hill was a patch of dirt surrounded by petrified fallen tree trunks. Rhan dropped the prince's arm and vaulted over one of the fallen trees.

Theo noticed the ring formed by the fossilized lumber. "What is this place?" he asked as he traced a hand across the sun-bleached bark.

"I made this training area when we first settled here last spring," Rhan smiled, "it was supposed to be a place for me to practice and hone my abilities. But Ahote and a handful of the tribe's warriors found it and turned it into a training ring."

Rhan reached up and adjusted her feathers downwards against the back of her neck. She unhooked the clasp holding her ceremonial shawl over her shoulders and let it slip to the ground. Underneath she wore a chest wrap and baggy pants that stopped halfway down her shins. Her arms, chest, and legs had black bands tattooed into her green-yellow skin.

"Are you coming?" Rhan asked. She craned her neck to one side and started bouncing on the ball of her feet, "that is unless you think I'll beat you up too badly?"

Theo felt the strike at his pride and instead of letting it wound him, he used it as fuel. "Alright," the prince agreed as he stepped into the dirt ring, "what's the game here? Three-point winner? Capture the flag?"

"First one to pin their opponent," Rhan answered.

"I'm not going to pin you," Theo argued.

"So you're scared?" Rhan poked.

"No," Theo burst out defensively, "I just—don't want to hurt you."

Rhan stepped up to the prince, staring him eye to eye, and smiled at him sarcastically.

Up until now, Theo hadn't noticed her size. Next to Ta'goda, she seemed small, but in front of Theo, she made *him* feel small. He glanced at her muscular shoulders and felt his confidence slowly leave his body.

"Are we going to fight, then?" Rhan pressured.

"Fine," Theo agreed sharply.

The two stepped back and went to opposite sides of the ring.

Theo unbuttoned his shirt and carefully laid it over one of the log barriers. He flexed and stretched every muscle he could think of before turning and facing Rhan.

She stared back at the prince with a devious smirk on one side of her face.

Theo rolled his shoulders back and bounced his way towards the center of the ring.

The two met in the middle and immediately collided. Rhan made the first move against an unsuspecting Theo, quickly spinning the prince around and kicking him square in the rear.

Theo stumbled forward a few steps before turning around and resetting himself.

"You sure you're ready?" Rhan teased.

Theo didn't respond. He moved closer, cautious of getting too close, and raised his arms in front of his chest.

Rhan purposely lowered her guard to taunt him with a free shot.

Theo leaped at the chance and swept the orc's legs out from under her. With a heavy thud, she slammed onto her back.

"Alright," Rhan grunted as she pulled herself up. Before

Theo could react, she grabbed him by the wrist and threw him over her shoulder.

Theo hit the dirt and all the air escaped his lungs. He lay there for a moment, trying to feel for broken or displaced bones. When he managed to regain his breathing, he jumped to his feet.

Rhan didn't give him time to prepare as she took three quick jabs at his shoulder. She lined up to strike his other shoulder but the prince jerked back and dodged the hit.

Theo took his momentum and spun backward towards Rhan. He took the back of his shoulder and body checked her from the side, causing her to stumble.

Back and forth the two sparred, each blow landing without malice or intent to injure. They started to sweat and their chests pounded with adrenaline. Theo felt like they had been dancing again, each countering the other's movements as they went around in circles.

Rhan maneuvered the prince in front of her and in one final blow, she dove headfirst into Theo's chest. She wrapped her arms around him and the two slammed onto the ground one last time. She quickly sat up with her hands pressed against Theo's shoulders. "That's a pin!" she cheered.

Theo laid in the dirt as Rhan got up and danced around the ring celebrating. After a couple of laps around the fallen prince, she turned back to him and knelt at his side.

"Deep breaths," she whispered calmly. She hovered a hand over Theo's chest and cradled the back of his neck with the other hand.

"I'm—fine," he grunted, trying to sit up. But there was a piercing pain in his side. Like a dagger deep beneath his flesh.

Rhan pushed him back down. "No, you're not," she told him. She took the hand that cradled his neck and ran her fingers along his side until Theo burst out with a wail of pain.

"Keep breathing," Rhan said, "you've got two ribs out of place."

"Gee, thanks," Theo grunted through his teeth.

Rhan held her hand over Theo's chest again, this time closing her eyes and slowing down her breathing as she did. Blue flames began to flicker from the sides of her hand and Theo felt the heat above his chest.

It didn't burn as she lowered her palm against the prince's bare skin and a warm sensation filled his lungs. He felt his chest expand and there was no more pain.

"What—did you do?" Theo groaned as she helped him sit up again.

"I set the two ribs for you," Rhan explained, lifting the prince to his feet. "I wasn't going to hurt you like that and not fix it."

"I would have—been alright," Theo tried to play it off. He stood up and walked over to where he left his shirt.

"I'm sure you would have," Rhan chuckled, "but there would have been lasting damage that might cause you issues later on."

Theo kept his eyes on the ground in embarrassment as he buttoned his shirt.

"That was quite some training though," Rhan complimented him. She stood up and dusted the front of her pants off. "It's been a while since someone was able to take me down like that."

"It's day one in our training," Theo responded, "if you take out the enemy at the legs, you'll have the advantage to—" he froze.

"It's the advantage to kill your opponent," Rhan finished for him. "I'm aware of your father's training. I've seen plenty of his men in combat before."

"You've been in battle?" Theo stiffened.

"As the future chief, I will have to lead my people in battle should we face it," Rhan said as she picked her shawl off the ground. "How could I ask anyone to lay their life down for the tribe if I myself wouldn't be the first one to do so?"

"I just—"

"You thought only our men would go to battle?" Rhan interrupted, "there's a lot you've been kept from while hidden in those walls you called home."

"So I'm learning," Theo chuckled, trying to lighten the tension building.

"Maybe, if you come back here someday, I can teach you some more," Rhan offered.

Theo's face went red hot.

"I could show you how to fight your enemy without killing them," she continued, fastening the pin to her shawl and walking over to Theo. She held her arm out to him.

He looked back at her confused. "Are you not going to escort me back to the feast?" she asked playfully.

The prince didn't react as he processed the gesture.

"Come on," Rhan laughed, wrapping herself around one of Theo's arms and leading him back down the trail.

MAN IN THE MASK

Theo and Rhan talked the entire hike back to camp. They laughed at each other's jokes, shared stories from their lives, and pondered what was to come. Together they bonded over their shared roles as future leaders and their anxieties of disappointing those they would one day lead.

"Do you think you'll ever return home?" Rhan asked cautiously.

"I hope so," Theo sighed, "but the longer I'm away, the less I want to."

"But what about your sister?" Rhan stopped and looked at him.

"There is nothing I want more than to see her to safety. Just like she did for me."

"It was a noble sacrifice for her to stay behind," Rhan sighed, "I've come to know her well through our letters."

"You know Alice?" Theo perked up.

"Not personally, no," Rhan shook her head, "but I would receive her letters for my father and translate them to him."

"You would translate? He already speaks perfectly."

"My father never learned to read," she said with a small chuckle. "He's gone through a lot in his life. He was named chief when he was younger than us."

Theo swallowed hard.

"Could you imagine, barely being old enough to make your own decisions as a person and having to do it for an entire tribe? Really makes you think," Rhan sighed whimsically.

It was something Theo thought about often. "Where did you learn to read?" he asked, trying to change the subject.

Rhan hesitated.

"I'm sorry, I didn't mean to—"

"No, you didn't—it's—it's a long story," Rhan assured him.

"We've got nothing but time," Theo said, gesturing at the rest of the trail between them and the camp.

Rhan didn't respond and Theo looked back at her. Her eyes were wide with fear as she stared at the sky behind him. Theo turned his head and watched two massive balls of firelight fall from the dark clouds over the trail ahead.

"What is that—" Before Theo could get another word out, screams erupted in the air, and Rhan burst into a sprint. She pushed past the prince, and Theo took off behind her.

Over the horizon, explosions lit up the night sky over the Woyan homes. Theo and Rhan ran straight into the camp through fleeing crowds escaping the maze of tents. Flashes of orange and red lit up the sky again and more screams echoed in the valley.

Theo stepped into the open area that had been filled with happy celebration only a little while ago and stood amongst fiery destruction. Blackened beams of wood stood together as the remaining canvas and leather walls charred into ash.

Woyan warriors clashed with armored beings in the midst of the devastation. The clanging of stone axes against steel shields rang between battle cries.

Rhan joined the battle with blue flames around her fists. She grabbed one of the armored beings and dragged him off the back of a Woyan warrior.

More warriors battled the armored soldiers to the ground and took their weapons before they could recover them.

Theo looked up to the sky as another massive ball of orange fire was hurled towards the center of camp. It exploded overhead, sending embers into the still-standing homes.

"Theo!"

The prince spun and saw Oli charging in his direction.

"Don't just stand there, we need to get out of here!"

Oli grabbed Theo by the arm and tried to pull him away from the battle, but the prince jerked himself free.

"What are you doing?" Oli shouted.

"I'm not leaving Rhan here!" Theo shot back. He grabbed a sword from the ground and went back to the fight. He searched for Rhan in the flurry of flashing steel as fire continued to erupt around him.

"Get out of here!" he heard Rhan shout.

"I'm not leaving you behind," Theo answered blindly, slamming his sword into a metal breastplate.

"No, you need to run!" a third voice, Jeb's voice, commanded.

"You might want this by your side," Nila's voice added into the mix.

Theo glanced over in time to see the elf toss a scabbard and saber. The pearl white handle and silver crossguard glinted against the firelight. He dropped the heavy sword in his hand and caught the flying saber with the other.

A broadsword came crashing into the dirt at his feet, narrowly missing the prince's face. Theo drew the saber from the sheath and lunged at the assailant.

The saber stabbed between two plates of armor and Theo could hear the soldier grunt in pain as he withdrew. Crimson coated the silver tip of the saber and reflected the flickering light. He had never been on a battlefield like this or harmed another being for the sake of his own life.

"Would you take him and get out of here!" Jeb's voice cut in again.

"I've got him!" Rhan snapped. She released her chokehold on one of the armored beings as they rag-dolled to the ground. The chief's daughter grabbed Theo by the wrist and pulled him away from the fight.

She led the prince to Oli and the three of them made their way back into the maze of tents. Rhan jumped over debris as she guided the two boys to safety.

Out of nowhere, an explosion rocked the ground and sent a large shadow flying in front of Rhan, stopping her in her tracks.

The shadow quickly evolved into Ta'goda rising out of a now-destroyed tent. He picked up a large axe from the ground and slammed the head against a shield that protected his other arm.

"Dad!" Rhan burst out.

Ta'goda turned his intense focus to his daughter and suddenly his entire body deflated.

Without another word between the two, Ta'goda stood up from his fighting stance, faced whatever was hiding from view of the other three, and he closed his eyes.

Around the towering orc, three snarling wolves made of green flame formed from the ground up. Ta'goda raised his axe in the direction of his fight and the wolves took off.

Once the wolves were out of sight, Ta'goda rushed to his daughter and wrapped her in his arms.

"Rhan," Ta'goda choked out.

"I'm okay," she cried into his shoulder.

The chief pulled away and looked her in the eyes.

"What happened?" Rhan asked as she wiped away tears from her cheeks.

"We are under attack," Ta'goda gritted his teeth, "I must get back to the battle. Our tribe needs me."

"And me—"

Ta'goda shook his head at Rhan's protest.

"What?" Rhan blinked at her father.

"You have a new duty," Ta'goda swallowed. The chief's eyes peered over his daughter's shoulders and locked onto Theo. "I cannot leave our people and get the prince to the rivers—"

"I'm not leaving you here—"

"Rhan'takono, this is not the time to argue—"

"There is nothing to argue over! I'm fighting beside you—"

"I can't—"

"I am to be chief one day! How can I stand before my people after running from this?"

"If you don't go now, there won't be a tribe for you to be chief of!" Ta'goda snapped. "This is not a command as your chief. I am begging you, as your father—" the words caught in the back of his throat, "please."

Rhan's shoulders dropped.

Ta'goda placed his hand on the back of his daughter's head and planted a kiss on her forehead. "We will see each other again, my child," he promised. Ta'goda stepped back from Rhan and faced down the way he had flown from. "Head east to the Riverlands. Find Mak'tae. He can get you there faster than any other—"

Another explosion ripped through the tents, clearing the entire camp.

Ta'goda, Rhan, Theo, and Oli were knocked off their feet. Wood tangled in canvas launched overhead and crashed into the dirt around them.

Theo, shaken from the blast, sat up and looked at the

burning field. Standing on the opposite side of the debris were three slender figures shrouded in shadow.

The two on the outside peeled off from the middle figure to join in the fight. Theo watched as the shadows mercilessly killed any warrior in their reach. He couldn't see the attacks, he only heard the final screams for mercy as their victims became prey.

As the two tore through the pockets of fighting, the third figure walked ominously towards Theo and his friends.

The prince started to crawl to his feet but something grabbed him by the ankle. He fought and struggled against the binding but it overpowered him. Theo was dragged through the dirt and left at the feet of the wandering third figure.

Panicking, Theo slashed with the saber still in his hand. The being shot their hand out and caught the silvery blade in their palm.

A flame roared nearby, illuminating the figure. Theo saw a man with ash-gray skin and long white hair beneath a dark cloak. He wore a black mask that covered the top half of his face revealing only his eyes and mouth.

The man knelt down next to Theo and reached into the breast of his cloak. He slowly produced a thin, smooth, black wand and pressed one end forcefully underneath the prince's chin.

"Here's the deal, Your Highness," the man's icy, emotionless words sent goosebumps down Theo's back, "you're going to come with me. I will bring you back to your father and we will act like none of this ever happened." He twisted the end of the wand with the tips of his fingers and it pinched the skin on Theo's chin. "*If—*" the man emphasized, "you give me any difficulty, I will paralyze you with a bolt of lightning through your brain, leaving you barely alive." He pressed the wand further into the prince's jaw.

The man looked away from Theo and over to the three

slowly moving bodies trying to get back up. An evil grin crawled beneath his mask and he carefully pulled the wand from Theo's chin. Pinching it between his thumb and first two fingers, he pointed it at Ta'goda.

"I'm going to let you ponder my instructions," the man said greasily, dropping the saber's blade. "I have more orders to fulfill."

With a flick of his wrist, a bolt of white lightning exploded from the end of the wand and struck Ta'goda's shoulder.

It sent the chief, a towering orc of muscle, flying through the burnt husks of homes he once protected.

"I hope you don't mind, Your Highness," the man jabbed, "it's just business."

He turned his hand over and pointed it at the ground. Pulling it towards him, Ta'goda's massive body was dragged through the mounds of debris and stopped at the man's feet.

The man stood over the chief and placed his boot against the orc's chest. Leaning down on his knee, he brushed the loose hair on Ta'goda's forehead with his wand.

"Chief," the man smirked. "Ta'goda, The Raging Bear. You and that little half-blood traitor over there are going to bring me quite some coin."

Ta'goda's jaw tightened in anger.

"Don't look so upset," the man shook his head, "you're worth more to me alive."

He spun his wand in a circle and Ta'goda struggled to get up. The chief couldn't move his arms from his sides or bend his knees.

"I wouldn't fight too hard," the man said as he stepped off Ta'goda's chest, "that binding gets tighter when you do." Without another word, he continued walking towards Rhan and Oli.

Theo rolled onto his side and got to his knees. "Stop!" the

prince shouted in anger, pushing up to his feet. He dragged his saber through the dirt and held it out in front of him.

The masked man froze in his tracks, spinning on his heels, and looking back at the prince.

"Do—not—touch them," Theo growled. The raw patches of skin on his back from being dragged in the rubble burned as his rage boiled inside. "I am your prince and I command you—"

"That's not how this works, kid," the man clipped, "I don't conform to your hierarchy. Your words mean nothing to me. The only thing that tells me what to do is the money and right now, your father is paying me quite a lot of money for the three of you." He slowly lifted his wand towards the prince.

Theo placed his right foot behind him and lifted his saber in front of his chest with both hands.

"I get everything he offered if I bring you home alive with both of them alive. There's a small cut of my pay if I bring you back dead but both of them alive," the man explained sharply. "I could, however, bring all three of you dead and your father will still pay me enough to retire for the remainder of my life." Another devilish smirk ripped across his face, "and believe me, I will live for quite a long time."

Theo stared the man down.

"I will give you to the count of three," the man said, "lay down the sword and get on your knees. One—two—ARHGGG!"

From behind, a wolf made of green flame dug its sharp teeth into the masked man's shoulder. The two flailed for a moment before two more fiery wolves ran in.

A burst of red light shot out of the man's wand and the first wolf's form dissipated from existence. Quickly, he retreated as the other wolves snapped and snarled trying to get a bite on him.

Theo moved to run at the man, but he stopped when he saw Ta'goda getting to his feet.

The chief rose with a burning green aura around his body. His muscles rippled as he let out a ferocious roar. Theo watched as the aura took form around Ta'goda's frame in the shape of a bear.

Ta'goda sprang into action and rushed the masked man who was distracted with the remaining wolves.

He tackled the man to the ground and they struggled in the dirt, hacking at each other. Ta'goda fought for the wand, making sure it never aimed at him.

"Theo," a woman's voice filled the prince's head. He looked over his shoulder but no one was there. "Sweetheart, you need to run!"

It was his mother's voice. He could hear her inside his head.

"Theo, listen to me," she begged, "I'm with you. I always will be, now run!"

Without hesitation, Theo's legs burst into a sprint. He ran towards the two men fighting, bolted around Ta'goda and the masked man, and he dropped in front of Oli. Theo forced Oli to his feet and carried him over his shoulders.

"Theo?" Oli mumbled, trying to steady himself.

"It's me," Theo said. He let his friend go and ran to help Rhan. "Come on," he grunted as he helped her get up.

Another burst of red light came from the masked man and Ta'goda was launched off the man.

Not stopping to assess the damage, the chief jumped at the man again, and delivered a massive headbutt into the mask.

Theo and Oli started to run, but Rhan stood frozen, watching her father fight. The two boys quickly grabbed her arms and begged her to flee.

"No, no! I won't leave him!" she screamed.

"We have to get out of here!" Theo shouted back as he wrapped his arms around her stomach to stop her from going to help. "He's giving us a chance to escape."

"No, no, no!" Rhan howled through tears.

Theo and Oli finally took the leverage against her and the three ran deep into the hills.

"Where are we going?" Oli grunted out as they carried the chief's daughter away.

"Ta'goda said—he said we needed to—" Theo tried to recall. "The Riv—Riverlands!" he remembered. "We were supposed to meet someone there. M—Mark—Mac—"

"Mak'tae!" Rhan shouted.

The boys stopped dragging her and she stood on her own.

"He'll meet us in the Riverlands—"

"No, Mak'tae isn't a person—" Rhan said through pained sniffling, "quick, follow me. We're going the wrong way!" She turned and raced in another direction.

"Where are we going?" Oli stood frozen.

"Shut up and follow her!" Theo yelled over his shoulder as he ran after Rhan.

She led the boys out of the main camp and leapt over a log fence that surrounded a dark mound in the open fields.

"Stay out there until I get him moving," Rhan instructed. She grabbed a woven mat off the fence and draped it over the mound in the middle of the pen. "Hey buddy," She said calmly as she nudged the mound gently. There was a soft animal-like response as the elongated shadow stood on four massive legs.

Rhan created a small flame with her hand for some light. A blue flicker illuminated the beast's snout. But it wasn't a nose for an animal this size, in fact, it wasn't a snout at all. There was a bright yellow beak with large eyes to match. White feathers outlined the facial features and spotted brown feathers ran across the rest of the massive beast's round body.

The owl-faced beast playfully brushed its cheek against Rhan, nearly knocking her over.

"Easy there, big guy," Rhan said, scratching the feathers underneath its chin. "I need you to wake up, we've got to ride."

The beast straightened its front legs and stretched backward. From deep within its chest the beast let out a low bear growl before a soft owl's hoot whistled from its beak.

Rhan turned back to the fence and lifted a large saddle onto the beast's back. "Have either of you ever ridden an owlbear?"

"I'm sorry?" Oli frowned.

"I take that as a no." She relit the flame in her hand and threw it at the fence. Torches all around the fence line lit up with a low flame.

The owl-faced beast was harnessed with the saddle on its bear-like body with brown and white feathers that matched the ones in Ta'goda's headdress.

Rhan grabbed a set of leather straps hanging off the fence post and buckled them around the owlbear's shoulders. It let out a grumpy groan as she tightened the straps.

"I know, I know," Rhan sighed. She took her hand and scratched its chest. "We don't have time for me to teach you guys, it's going to be difficult with the three of us on Mak'tae. He usually only carries one or two people but Dad's about the size of both of you, I think he'll manage—"

Rhan froze and started twitching.

"Rhan!" Theo and Oli screamed.

She lifted off her feet and spun towards the boys. They could tell she was being strangled but nothing was touching her.

"If either of you moves—" the familiar icy voice of the masked man sent chills down both their spines, "I won't hesitate to kill her. When I tell you to, you're going to turn towards me and lay down your arms."

Theo stared at Rhan, his chest pumping with fear as he watched the life being squeezed out of her.

"Alright," the man clipped, "half-blood—turn!"

Theo and Oli looked at each other.

"Turn around!" the man shouted impatiently in anger.

Oli slowly turned.

"I want you to take the sword from him," the man ordered.

Oli looked at the prince and then down at his hand. Trying not to lose sight of the masked man, Oli leaned over and took Theo's saber.

"Good," the man's slimy voice oozed from his mouth, "now throw it towards me."

Oli stared down at the pearl handle before hesitantly tossing the saber in the dirt.

"Now, Prince George—"

"It's Theo!" Oli snapped at the man.

The sound of a whip cracked and Oli dropped to his knees.

"Did I tell you to speak?" the man asked with a calm intensity.

Oli let out a horrifying scream.

"Stop it!" Theo demanded at the top of his lungs. His legs quickly spun him around to face the man. He winced, expecting to be attacked but the man just stared him down.

"What are you going to do?" the man smiled.

Theo took a step forward.

"I wouldn't do that if I were you," the man warned. He turned the wand in his hand and Oli burst out screaming again.

"STOP!" Theo begged. His throat burning with anger.

The man raised his other arm and turned his hand in the air. Rhan began choking harder behind Theo.

"I'll do whatever you want, just stop!" Theo cried, dropping to his knees in defeat.

The man didn't lower his hands. "Get up and come to me—"

"I don't think so!" a voice boomed.

Theo looked up just in time to see Jeb and Nila coming to the rescue. Jeb, with his guitar in his hands, strummed a chord that filled the entire valley. A purple shockwave shot out from the strings and slammed into the masked man like a wall of force.

Nila, still running alongside Jeb, hurled three daggers at the man. The first one landed short in the dirt while the other two caught him in the same shoulder.

Theo heard Oli and Rhan gasp for air as the man's spells were broken. The prince turned to his friend and helped him to his feet. He ushered Oli over the fence and took cover in the pen. Oli cautiously approached Mak'tae while Theo aided Rhan.

Colorful explosions of magic burst in the field as Jeb and the masked man volleyed spells back and forth. Nila drew her bow and began firing arrows at the man. "Head east, we'll cover you!" she shouted over her shoulder as an arrow glanced off the man's mask.

ESCAPE TO THE RIVERLANDS

Nila and Jeb continued battling the masked man, giving Rhan, Oli, and Theo a chance to escape. Rhan managed to finish attaching the reins as Mak'tae trotted away from the fight with the three on his back. The owlbear quickly picked up speed and powerfully charged over the hills of the plains.

Theo, sandwiched between Oli and Rhan, looked back over his shoulder. He could still see the dim light of the burning camp on the horizon.

"How far is it to the rivers?" Oli shouted against the wind whistling in their ears.

"If Mak'tae can keep this pace, we would be there in a couple of hours. Eventually, he's going to have to stop for water and rest. I'd say we'll make it after sunrise."

Theo could see a shadow in the far distance cutting through the moonlight. It looked like a cloud of black smoke and it was getting closer to them. The prince squinted at the shadow, hoping it would vanish, but it kept closing in on them.

"We've got company!" Theo yelled.

The others turned and saw the trail of smoke.

"What is that?" Oli asked.

"I'm not—"

A bolt of lightning erupted from the black cloud and narrowly missed the three on the owlbear. The bolt smashed into a stone outcropping in the dirt and sent shards of rock everywhere.

"Is that him?" Theo shouted.

Another bolt shot out, this time landing short, and sending a haze of dirt in the air behind them.

"He's trying to kill us!" Oli panicked.

"Come on!" Rhan gritted her teeth as she heeled Mak'tae's sides.

The owlbear pushed himself for a short burst before slowing up from overexerting his energy.

"She fed you feast scraps again, didn't she?" Rhan growled in frustration at the beast.

Theo and Oli watched the cloud gain ground on them.

"What do we do when he catches us?" Oli asked nervously.

"I still have my—" Theo stopped mid-sentence as he remembered what happened to his mother's saber. Hoping it would magically appear on his hip, he patted his belt.

There it was, sheathed and bouncing against his side. He wrapped his hand around the handle and felt the smooth pearl hilt. He looked down and saw the silvery crossguard on his belt.

A third bolt of lightning cracked beneath Mak'tae's feet and sent the owlbear tumbling forward in the dirt. Rhan, Oli, and Theo were launched from the owlbear's back and landed hard on the ground.

The black cloud snaked its way to the crash and the masked man stepped out in his full form. "Tsk, tsk, tsk," he clicked his tongue, looking around at the three on the ground. "You are becoming quite a pain in my ass." He stepped towards the prince and gave him a sharp kick in the ribs.

Theo wrapped himself around the man's legs and pulled his ankles out from under him.

The man hit the ground hard and Theo scrambled away.

"You little son of a bitch!" the man hissed. He rolled over and got up on his feet, drawing his wand from inside the breast of his cloak, he flicked the end of the wand towards the prince.

Theo turned to the man and drew his saber again.

"I thought I told you to get rid of that!" The man shouted in anger.

He slashed his wand through the air and Theo felt the sword being forced out of his hands. The prince gripped the handle tightly as it yanked him violently from side to side.

"Enough of this!" the man snarled. He turned his wand towards Oli and Rhan.

Theo anticipated the man's move. Shaking with fear, he jumped in front of his friends, and he raised the saber at the man.

The masked man's jaw tightened with rage as he raised his wand at the prince.

Theo swallowed and closed his eyes. He took a deep breath and waited.

TWANG!

Theo winced at the noise, expecting to be dead. He opened one eye to see a bloodied Jeb standing over the masked man's body. In his hand was the splintered neck of his guitar.

Jeb took two fingers and put them between his teeth. A shrill whistle screeched into the midnight air and seconds later, a tall rider on the back of a massive beast like Mak'tae galloped out of the shadows. It was Nila riding on the back of a horse-sized mastiff.

She pulled the reins on the towering canine and it stopped just short of plowing over Jeb. Nila climbed down off the dog's back with a coil of rope and started tying the masked man up. In seconds, she had the man folded together with his wrists strapped to his ankles.

Jeb dropped the broken half of his guitar on the ground and ran over to Theo. "Hey, kid," the small man smiled up at the prince. There were patches of blood and dirt beneath his white hairline. His left eye was swollen and the lower corner of his lip was split with a trail of blood down his chin. "Don't worry about me," he said cheerfully, "get those two moving again. Nila and I will be right behind—"

"Jeb!" Nila shouted.

Theo looked over and saw her struggling with the masked man who was quickly regaining consciousness.

"Go!" Jeb yelled as he shoved Theo away and ran to help. Purple, shining, ethereal ropes flung from Jeb's wrists and reinforced Nila's binding.

Theo rushed to Oli and rolled him onto his knees.

"I've—I've got it," Oli pushed up on his side, "get Rhan."

Theo crawled over to Rhan but she wasn't in the dirt.

"Get up!" he heard her voice. "Mak'tae, come on, get up!"

He looked to his right and saw Rhan shoving the unresponsive owlbear's back. She lit her hands up with the blue flames and put them against Mak'tae's feathers. Instantly, the owlbear's ribs expanded with life.

"Thank the ancestors," Rhan exhaled with relief. She helped the massive beast up to his feet and adjusted the saddle. Rhan turned back to the boys still laying in the dirt. "Get up!" She commanded.

Theo and Oli fumbled around as they raced over to her. The three of them climbed onto the owlbear's back and Rhan heeled his sides.

Mak'tae lurched forward, trying to run, but he let out a pained growl and dropped to the ground again with a defeated chirp.

Theo glanced back at Jeb and Nila as they fought to restrain the masked man.

Off to the side of the fight, the mastiff snarled and barked viciously.

"Sîta!" Nila shouted over her shoulder while rolling with the masked man in a chokehold.

The mastiff stopped barking and raised its head to scan the field. Its massive brown eyes caught Theo's and the dog jumped in the air. It barreled towards Theo, sliding through the dirt and stopping next to the downed owlbear.

Rhan climbed off the owlbear and knelt down in front of Mak'tae's beak. She pressed her forehead against the white patch of feathers between Mak'tae's eyes.

Theo and Oli quickly got down from Mak'tae's back. Theo helped Oli climb the mastiff's back.

The owlbear gave a sad hoot as it nuzzled against Rhan's cheek. She pulled her head back and stared into the beast's eyes. She mumbled something through tears to the owlbear and kissed him on the top of his head. She unbuckled Mak'tae's saddle and stepped back.

The owlbear looked at Rhan one last time before shaking free of the saddle and trotting off in a different direction. He limped out of view, vanishing into the night.

Crackling explosions and snapping sounds echoed through the valley as Jeb and Nila took defensive positions against the masked man.

Theo helped Rhan up onto the mastiff and he took her hand as he climbed after her.

The horse-sized dog looked back at the three on its back and then to the colorful battle behind them. It gave a sad whimper, turned away, and ran.

Sailing through the hills as if they didn't exist, the mastiff ran through the night. It ran for miles before trotting another few miles. When they were safe, the canine slowed to a walk. They rode for an hour without looking back and Rhan led the dog to a nearby creek where all four of them drank till their stomachs hurt.

The mastiff curled up against the largest tree and fell asleep in a matter of seconds.

Oli propped himself against the giant canine and closed his eyes. He fought the urge to sleep, jumping awake every time his head rolled away. But eventually, he got comfortable and gave in to his weariness.

Theo sat on the creek bed with his mother's saber. He stared at the red stain now dried on the silver tip. The moonlight reflected off the blade, giving it a soft white glow.

He flipped the saber and held the handle up to the light. Running his thumb along the smooth, yellowish-white pearl hilt, he wondered what was special about this blade. He thought about how it always came back to him since his sister handed it to him in the castle on the morning of their mother's funeral.

He clutched the handle tightly in his hand with the blade pointed away from him. Letting the weight of the saber bend his wrist.

"Theo," his mother's voice echoed in his head.

He froze as chills ran down his spine. The sound of trickling water and chirping bugs filled the air. He looked around and saw Oli still curled up with the furry mastiff. Rhan sat at the edge of the small thicket of aspens and stared over the plains.

Theo stood from the creekbank, slid the saber into its sheath, and carefully walked towards Rhan. As he got closer, he heard soft whimpering stifled by an occasional sniffle.

"Rhan?"

She quickly tucked her face into her arm and tried to clean up the tears. "Ye—ehem—yeah?"

"Are you alright?" Theo asked cautiously.

Rhan pulled her face from the bend of her arm and sat up, still facing the other direction. "I'm fine."

He could hear her battling down her emotions. Something about it reminded him of Ta'goda's stoicism.

"I—he was—I wish—"

Rhan shook her head. The feathers still tucked into her braids swung side to side. "You don't have to say anything," she choked out, "it's alright."

Theo swallowed dryly.

"My father always taught me that a good leader knew when the time for words and action was," she paused as a knot formed in her throat, "but a *great* leader knew when to sit and listen."

"That's all I want to do," Theo said nervously as he lowered himself beside her.

"Right now," Rhan sighed, "I want a little rest." She turned towards Theo, keeping her face hidden in the shadows of the trees. "There's a lot of ground to cover before we're in the Riverlands. If we still have a tail, they'll be here in no less than an hour if they aren't already here." She glanced down at the sheathed saber dangling on the prince's hip. "You'll want to clean that before you tarnish the steel."

Theo gave her a confused frown before looking down and realizing what she was talking about. "R—right," he nodded.

Rhan rushed past the prince and carried on about her business.

Theo stayed where he was for a while. Leaning against a tree, he decided he needed some rest.

Making the best of where he was, Theo fashioned a blanket out of a cloak he found in a saddle pack and propped himself up against another tree.

He took the saber out and examined the stain again. He held his hand up from under the cloak, setting the tip of the blade in his palm on the other side of the fabric, folded it over the steel, and wiped away at the blood.

It took him a couple of passes but eventually, the blade was restored to its former shine. When he was satisfied, Theo put the saber away and leaned back into the tree trunk.

His mind quickly drifted off and in minutes he was asleep. Everything vanished and for what felt like hours to his weary, unconscious mind, the prince escaped to the endless void of dreamless sleep.

"Theo, wake up," his mother's voice interrupted his heavy slumber. "Sweetheart, you need to get up."

In his dazed, half-awake state, Theo thought he was home again. He began to stir, anticipating waking up in his bed with his mother sitting next to him.

"Theo, get up. You're not safe here," his mother's voice echoed in his head again, "they're coming."

Theo furrowed his brow in confusion as he sat up. He blinked his eyes open cautiously as his vision cleared. There was no sunlight at all. He looked around and saw the nature surrounding him was still shrouded in the dark of night.

Theo tried to stand but when he moved his arms to push off the dirt, the saber was in his hand.

"Didn't I—" Theo mumbled to himself. He stared at the silver steel for a brief second and then slid it into the scabbard.

Using the tree, Theo climbed to his feet and stretched his arms high over his head.

In the distance, a glint of light caught the prince's attention. He squinted, trying to see as far as he could but it was too dark.

There was another flicker that was quickly followed by another a little further up. Whatever it was it was moving quickly and it was moving towards them just as fast.

"You need to run!" the bodiless voice of his mother whistled in his ear like a howling wind.

"Oli! Rhan!" Theo called his friends. "They found us!"

Both of them burst out of their sleep and jumped to their feet ready to fight. Their groggy state quickly faded and they raised their guard.

Theo ran over to them and tucked the cloak back into its saddlebag.

Rhan quickly got the mastiff ready and the three of them rode off into the rolling hills as far as the mastiff could carry them. While the dog lapped water out of every creek it stopped at, Theo, Rhan, and Oli stood watch.

The first few stops ended after they caught the slightest glimpse of the shining light on the horizon. After a few hours of traveling and a handful more breaks, the four came to a deep cliff canyon.

The mastiff stopped short of the ledge and let its riders down.

In the east, the early rays of sunrise painted the sky. The dark blues and blacks became shades of purples and oranges.

Oli pulled out a waterskin they found in the mastiff's saddlebag and filled at the last creek. He pulled the cap off and offered the opening to the mastiff. Water trickled out onto the dog's spotted tongue.

Rhan interrupted the trickle with her hands cupped together. When her palms filled, she raised them to her lips, and slowly sipped as she wandered over to the cliff edge of the canyon.

Theo waited for his turn to drink. He let the water stream down his tongue and it cooled the stinging burn in the back of his throat before dropping into his empty stomach.

"Nat'an, mohey!" Rhan shouted into the canyon. Her voice echoed between the tall walls of red rock.

"P'lote san mevah!" A voice responded.

Theo and Oli looked at each other before both racing over to see who Rhan was talking to. When the boys peered over the ledge, they saw dozens of beings camped out on both banks of a wide river that cut through the monumental canyon.

A large orc man stood near the wall, away from his camp, and was looking up at them with his hands around the edges of his mouth.

"Who is that?" Theo asked.

"This is my cousin, Nat'an," Rhan answered with a smile, "*Chief* Nat'an."

RIVER WOLF

Nat'an and a group of beings from the camp below quickly hiked the natural trail that wound up the canyon wall. Nat'an rushed to Rhan and wrapped her in a massive, welcoming hug.

"I'm so glad you made it here safely," Nat'an greeted Rhan as he pulled back to look at her. "What happened to you? Have you been fighting wild beasts out on the prairie without me?"

Theo noticed Nat'an's precise pronunciations. He didn't carry an accent like Ta'goda or Rhan and he spoke clearer than Jeb or Nila.

"I wish that were the case," Rhan sighed.

Nat'an quickly caught the hidden pain in her words, "Whatever happened, we will get through it together as a family." Nat'an moved his hand to the back of her neck and pressed his forehead against hers.

The rest of Nat'an's group circled the boys and the mastiff with clay jugs of water. They offered the sloshing vases to the prince and filled their waterskins.

Nat'an turned from his cousin and walked over towards Theo. He stood nearly two heads taller than the prince and he had a striking resemblance to Ta'goda. A much younger, leaner Ta'goda.

Nat'an's bonnet was much smaller than his uncle's. A messy bundle of brownish-red feathers were tucked into a tight bun on the top of his head and a silver ring dangled from inside his nose through the septum, with matching earrings hanging from his earlobes. On his cheek beneath his right eye were three, small, red triangles tattooed in a line, all pointing down. Behind his left ear were two elongated blue triangle tattoos that stretched down the side of his neck.

Nat'an looked Theo up and down before giving him a disappointed smile. He stood in front of the prince and folded his arms across his chest. "I hope I'm not being rude," Nat'an spoke, "but you are not the princess."

Theo's swallowed nervously, "My name—"

"I already know who you are," Nat'an cut him off, "most of the world knows who *you* are." He unfolded his arms and bowed his head, "I must offer you my condolences. The loss of your mother has left a hole in this world that will not be easily filled."

"You knew my mother?" Theo asked as a chill ran down his spine.

"A story—I am afraid—for another time," Nat'an continued, "I should, however, introduce myself." He stepped back, addressing both Theo and Oli. Pounding a fist against his chest with a proud smile, he stood tall and presented himself. "I am Nat'an Usato, Chief of the Okota tribe. I am known to my people as The River Wolf," he said, lowering his fist to his side, "but in the city, they call me Nate."

Theo blinked at the new chief as he processed the information.

"Again, I will have to explain later," Nat'an said, "I am glad you all made it early. We will wait for the rest of the party before setting sail—"

"Nat'an..." Rhan cut in, her voice cold.

Without another word, Nat'an nodded. He looked to the group that stood around the massive mastiff, petting and playing with it. "Head back to the camp, wake everyone, and get the canoes ready. We are setting off," the chief instructed.

All but one of the beings in the crowd broke off from the mastiff and headed back down the trail. The remaining being, an orc boy a few years younger than Theo, held the reins and led the dog behind the group into the canyon.

Nat'an turned to Oli and gestured to let him go first, "I do apologize, I never asked your name."

Oli's jaw was tight and his ears pointed straight like arrows. "It's Oli."

"Oli," Nat'an echoed, "is that short for—"

"Olsdeyr," Oli clipped.

Nat'an caught the sharp answer and chuckled to try to break the tension. "Is that elvish?"

Oli shrugged and started walking after the boy and the dog.

Nat'an frowned.

"He's been through a lot," Theo said, "*we've*— been through a lot together."

Nat'an nodded and looked back at Theo and Rhan. He straightened himself, "I assume your father will be joining us soon?"

Rhan's shoulders sank.

Nat'an's eyes darted to Theo's, filled with concern. But then he looked past the prince.

Theo turned around and saw a familiar feathered mound hobbling at them from the horizon. He grabbed Rhan by the shoulder and shook her until she looked.

"Mak'tae?" she burst out tearfully.

Both of them ran to the owlbear and Nat'an followed.

As Theo got closer and could see Mak'tae's features, he also saw two bodies slumped over his back. "Jeb! Nila!" The names escaped his lips like a breath being pulled from his lungs as he saw the two unconscious faces. He ran to their side and carefully pulled Jeb down from beneath Nila.

Nat'an quickly jumped around Theo and grabbed Nila. Effortlessly, he got her over his shoulder and gently onto the ground. Theo laid Jeb next to Nila.

Both of them were covered in dried blood, dirt, bruises, and a number of scars. If it weren't for the very faint breathing, Theo would have thought they were dead.

Jeb clutched the broken neck of his guitar with Ta'goda's headdress in one hand and the chief's pipe, broken in two, in his other hand. Blood stained the feathers and the colorful beads woven into the headband. Theo looked over to Rhan as she was struggling to heal Mak'tae's beak.

"To-katae, to-katae," She grunted in frustration as the owlbear winced and moved away from her hands, "mona ta-tea."

Theo opened his mouth to call her but he felt a hand grabbing his wrist. He whipped his head back towards Jeb and saw him starting to blink his eyes open.

"He—hey kid," he let out weakly, "long time, no—" he started coughing in pain. "You already—know." He tried to chuckle but it triggered another fit of coughing.

Theo smiled back and felt tears trailing down his cheek.

"I'm—excited to see you too—kid," Jeb choked out. "But—you've got to get out of—here"

A howl echoed from far across the hills causing the hairs on the back of Theo's neck to stand on end.

"They're coming," Jeb grunted. He tried to sit up but was too weak. "Where's R—Rhan?"

Theo looked back for Rhan but she wasn't yelling at Mak'tae. She was standing behind Theo in shock as she stared at the bloodied headdress and broken pipe clutched in Jeb's fists. She dropped to her knees, running her fingers across the brown feathers.

Another bone-chilling howl cried into the morning sky.

"Rhan," Nat'an said, placing a hand on her shoulder.

She gave a small nod, took the artifacts from Jeb's hands, and stood.

Nat'an scooped Nila in his arms and followed behind Rhan. Theo tried to get Jeb over his shoulder but wasn't successful without hurting him.

"I—got it, kid," Jeb groaned. He raised his hand and swirled it over his head. Out of nowhere, a giant purple hand made of ethereal energy lifted Jeb out of the dirt and carried him away.

Theo watched in astonishment for a brief moment before a much closer howl rang in his ears. The prince sprang to his feet and chased after the rest of the group.

Nat'an lead them down the cliffside, being as cautious as he could going this quickly. They regrouped with the rest of the tribe in the canyon along the riverbanks.

Theo saw the canoes and couldn't believe his eyes. Long, hand-carved, and painted with stories on the outer hulls. There were five canoes that were ten people long. Two on each bank of the canyon river and one tethered between the lead canoes. Behind the tethered canoe was a pontoon boat kept afloat by two large buoys underneath a platform.

Theo's astonished state was quickly broken by the excited barking of the massive mastiff now charging in his direction. The beast of a dog slammed to a halt and slid to a stop just before plowing Theo and Jeb over. The mastiff violently licked Jeb's face as Theo tried to hold it back.

"Easy, girl, easy," Jeb chuckled through the pain. He tried to push the dog back with Theo but she was too big for either of them. "Rosa, down girl!" Jeb finally commanded.

The giant mastiff snapped to attention before lowering herself calmly to the ground.

"Good—mmph—girl," Jeb grunted out as he tried to reach out and pet her. After a couple of pats, Theo and Jeb turned to the river and Rosa followed closely.

One of the tribe's people in the back canoe, an older man with a thick, wiry, black beard and two small horns on his forehead helped Theo load Jeb onto the boat before getting in with both of them.

The man pushed off towards the pontoon and floated them next to the platform. When they were across the water, Theo got out onto the pontoon and turned back to get Jeb.

"Let me help," someone said as they reached down and grabbed Jeb's arm.

Theo looked up and saw Oli standing over him. He didn't look back at the prince but pulled Jeb up onto the platform.

The man in the canoe continued drifting between the boat and riverbank, transporting the rest of the group.

First Rhan with a still unconscious Nila, followed by a hesitant mastiff who wouldn't sit still. Mak'tae struggled to hold his balance and needed lots of help getting in and out of the canoe, but he remained absolutely motionless while they floated to the pontoon.

As soon as Nat'an stepped off the bank and into the canoe, the rest of the tribe filled the open spaces of the five boats.

Two different howls echoed through the canyon. Before Theo could look for them, a massive explosion burst from the cliff wall behind him.

Sharp boulders fell into the river, sending waves that rocked the pontoon violently. Theo missed a step trying to catch his balance and tripped into Mak'tae's side.

The prince scrambled to get off the owlbear and look for where the attack was coming from.

High up the canyon wall were three humanoid figures. The one standing taller than the other two pointed down at the river and an arc of lightning shot out from their hand, striking the riverbank in front of Theo.

"Cana'toa! Mwatan mor'ro!" Nat'an shouted as chunks of brittle stone rained down on top of the tribe.

Theo looked to the Okota Chief as he whipped his arms out in front of himself. From inside his fists, two ropes made of water flew out over the boats and landed downstream like fishing lines. He yanked on his ends of the water and it morphed the river's surface. The stream started to break as bulges transformed into an entire pack of wolves connected by harnesses of water. Nat'an gave the liquid reins another tug and the wolves splashed to life. The pack took off downstream, pulling all six boats behind them.

Another lightning bolt exploded in the water just behind the pontoon as it skidded across the river's surface.

Nat'an steered the pack of dogs through the winding turns of the canyon river and they sailed across calm waters as if they were white rapids.

Bolt after bolt of deadly electricity slammed into the monumental, red walls around them. The two shorter beings lost their pursuit shortly after the second turn but the larger being continued the chase at an inhuman speed. Theo watched as the being jumped into the canyon as their form shifted into a solid black cloud of smoke that tailed the speeding boats. Gaining on the water-wolf-drawn pontoon, a familiar torso and head appeared in the smoke. It was the masked man.

"Your Highness!" Theo heard Oli call out.

He spun around just in time to catch a harpoon spear Oli tossed at him. "What do I—" Theo tried to ask as Oli kicked another harpoon off the deck with his foot, caught it over his shoulder, and hurled it at the masked man's smoking figure.

The man dodged the spear and it splashed in the water behind the boat.

Theo got to his feet and hoisted the harpoon onto his shoulder. It was much heavier than Oli made it look. He struggled to get his grip while focusing on not falling off the back of the boat.

BOOM!

Another burst of lightning hit the canyon wall and a giant boulder crashed on top of the water-wolves pulling the boats. Unable to avoid the obstacle, Nat'an whipped the reins downwards and slammed them into the platform of the boat.

The river swelled beneath the pontoon, lifting the entire boat over the boulder in the middle of the stream. Once they were clear, the water formed into a wave that propelled the river fleet further down the canyon.

Nat'an stood back up and gave his reins another whip. As the water arched, the wolves appeared again and continued pulling the boats.

They increased the distance between themselves and the smoking figure of the masked man. He continued to volley bolt after bolt but only caught the water or canyon walls behind them.

Nat'an turned and looked over his shoulder with a smile. "I think we can lose him up here—"

The pontoon lurched in the air and came crashing back into the river. Theo dropped his harpoon, lost his footing, and slipped off the back end of the platform into the river.

"Theo!" Oli screamed as he dove for the prince, missing his hand as he went overboard.

"Rhan!" Nat'an called out.

Without more than a glance between each other, Rhan threw herself overboard after Theo.

Oli watched as a giant eagle made of blue flame amassed under her just before she hit the water and lifted her above the river. She leaned off the side of the eagle's back and reached down for Theo who was flapping his arms over the river.

The prince fought and struggled against the river's light current but it was too deep for him to have any control. His head bobbed in and out making it hard to catch a breath before he was submerged again.

Rhan managed to get a grip on Theo's wrist on the first pass and she tried to drag his body from the river. His torso was almost free of the water when the eagle pulled up sharply. Theo's wet arms slipped from Rhan's hands and he was swept away by the river again.

Rhan saw the black cloud of smoke blow past her on the eagle and the man reached down for Theo in the water.

She laid back against the eagle and let herself slide off its tail. Pointing her arms above her head towards the water, Rhan fell from the sky towards the man in the cloud.

Right before the man could snatch Theo by the collar, Rhan slammed into his back. His entire body was yanked from the smoke that now dissipated over the river. The two of them splashed into the water violently, vanishing beneath the surface.

In a panic, Theo tried his hardest to swim with the water's current. Another hand grabbed him by his collar and yanked him out of the water.

It was Nat'an. He was mounted on one of the water-wolves that stood on the surface of the moving river as if it was solid ground. Theo pulled himself onto the wolf's back with the help of Nat'an and the wolf carried them after the pontoon.

"What about Rhan?" Theo shouted over the splashing.

"She's protected by the ancestors," Nat'an answered as they caught up to the boat, "she will make it out of there."

The chief hoisted Theo onto the moving pontoon and climbed up himself. When he got to his feet, Theo saw Oli manning the reins.

"Olsdeyr, try to hold as center as you can!" Nat'an commanded. He was staring into the sky behind them, "these canyons begin to wind through tight passages. Not a lot of water to maneuver through."

Without another word, Nat'an threw an arm in the air, and with a blast of wind, the blue-flame eagle swooped over the boat. The massive bird wrapped its taloned feet around Nat'an's arm and pulled him into the air.

Theo watched the chief climb the eagle's side and carefully saddle himself on its back. They soared for a few seconds above the canyon before the eagle folded in its wings. The two dove straight down towards the river.

The eagle flared out its wings before hitting the water, snatched something under the river's surface, and with a powerful burst, the eagle shot out of the canyon again with Rhan dangling in its claws.

UNDER THE MOON

Nat'an flew the eagle behind the pontoon and gently landed after setting Rhan on her feet. Wasting no time, he got down and took the reins from Oli as the eagle's fiery form vanished on the platform.

"Are you alright?" Rhan grabbed Theo.

"What—I'm fine. Are *you* okay?"

Rhan gave him a small, distracted nod. "Find a secure spot and hold on tight. We can't afford to lose you overboard." She ushered Theo over to the small storage den in the floor of the platform where Mak'tae and Rosa were secured.

"You don't have to get in there with them, but hold onto the handles until we get out of the canyon," Rhan instructed.

Theo didn't argue and wrapped one of the ropes secured to the deck around his arm and held tight.

The pontoon continued racing downstream until Nat'an was sure he'd lost the masked man. Every so often, he commanded a barrel be thrown overboard into the river and Rhan would toss a ball of blue fire onto the barrel in the water. When the fire burned a hole into the exterior, the barrels would blow up behind them.

Nat'an exploded ten barrels into the water before they escaped the canyon's tight passage into a valley of dry, yellow grasses and sandy soil. The canyon's walls separated and created two long-peaked mountains that bordered the valley and faded off across different horizons.

They followed the river well into the evening and the sun began to set in front of them. As darkness blanketed the sky over the mountains, Nat'an led the tribe to a small marsh on the riverbank where they set up a camp for the night.

The tribe quickly pulled the canoes from the water and put together rain canopies between a small thicket of aspen trees a little distance from the riverbank. Eventually, they built a small camp around a decent fire.

Oli went off with Nat'an and a few of the Okota to fish in the river while the rest stayed back to tend to the wounded.

A handful of the canoe riders had been caught by flying debris in the attack; none of them severely hurt but with some cuts, bruises, and a few broken bones.

Rhan quickly got to work organizing those who remained in the camp and set up a small healing circle. She instructed and helped those who needed it and when the tribe had their jobs, she moved to Jeb.

He was propped against Mak'tae and Rosa was curled up behind them with the still unconscious Nila cradled against the mastiff's body.

Rhan silently knelt down and focused on Jeb's ribs.

"Hey—mph—kid," Jeb grunted to Theo as Rhan applied pressure to his abdomen.

"What happened?" Theo asked, sinking into the owlbear's coat of feathers next to Jeb. The prince felt his aching knees as he lowered himself to the ground.

"The bastard broke my—uhg—guitar," Jeb winced as Rhan pressed on his side. "He's dangerous," he warned soberly before reaching into his torn vest and pulling out a small, rolled pouch. He handed it to Theo with a smile, "do me a favor and unroll that for me?"

Theo opened the pouch in his lap and inside was a wooden pipe, a small black pouch, and a silver flask.

Jeb reached over with a shaky hand and pulled the flask from the pouch. He struggled to unscrew it with his fingers, but got it open, and took a long swig before offering it to Theo.

The prince looked at the silver canister hesitantly.

"It's okay to say no, kid," Jeb let out as he finished swallowing. "I don't blame you, this stuff is also dangerous."

Theo took the flask and pulled a small sip. The smoky flavor quickly turned to fire in his throat and he started to choke.

"Breathe," Jeb chuckled, "let it go down."

Theo inhaled and quickly let it out with a small gasp. He controlled his breathing and started to notice the cinnamon taste that now lingered in his mouth. "What—what is that stuff?" Theo choked out, feeling the velvet coating in his throat for the first time.

"This is my family's elixir. They call it Sweetbark Whiskey," Jeb explained with the flask held high and proud. He took another swig and offered it to Rhan. She took the flask and threw her head back.

"Easy there," Jeb stopped her after the fourth massive swallow. "That flask is enchanted and you'll drown yourself before it gets you drunk."

Rhan swallowed one last gulp before returning the flask to Jeb.

"My family has been distilling—hngh—for thousands of— oww—years," Jeb grunted as Rhan shifted down to his swollen knee. "Each generation adds their—brew into the family collection. That specific drink was my great-great-grandfather, Titus' batch. Aged for six-hundred years in a smoked elder—hmph—wood barrel."

Rhan moved her hands to Jeb's black eye and touched it gently with her fingers. The swelling deflated and Jeb was nearly back to his regular self with the exception of a handful of small cuts.

He took another drink from the flask, capped it, and tucked it into his vest. "I appreciate that," he nodded to Rhan. Carefully using Theo as support, Jeb got to his feet and stretched.

"You'll want to take it easy for the night," Rhan told him as she stood, towering over both Jeb and Theo.

Jeb turned and looked at Nila. Her slender, elven frame looked weak and frail under the pale moon. Dried blood clumped in her hair and trailed from every cut on her body. Her lip was split and part of her left ear looked like a wolf had bitten into it.

"What do you think, Doc?" Jeb sighed.

"It's going to take some time," Rhan frowned. She ran her hand over Mak'tae's back, causing the owlbear to coo and vibrate with joy. "I'm going to have Nat'an take a look at her. He might be able to flush out whatever is inside of her." Rhan looked down at Jeb, "what did he do to her?"

Jeb's shoulders sank and he shook his head. "Whatever kind of twisted magic he wields is deadly. He never once touched her physically but she floated in the air like she was possessed. It was almost as if she was withering away slowly but he wouldn't let her die." His voice started to shake, "it's been a long time since I've fought like this. He doesn't hold back."

Jeb didn't take his eyes off Nila. "He's after you, kid," Jeb continued, "he's hunting you and he won't stop until he does. Those other two, the lycanthropes with our hunter friend, are tracking your scent. It's only a matter of time before they pick it up again."

Theo didn't answer. He looked at Jeb confused but he didn't turn.

"Lycans are cursed beings," Jeb explained, feeling the confusion coming from the prince. "You'll hear a thousand tales about where they came from, each culture has one. But wherever it did come from, it mutates these people. Gives them the abilities of beasts."

Theo stiffened. He'd heard stories of beasts roaming during full moons. Another fairytale he couldn't have imagined being true.

"It will take them a while to find our trail," Nat'an inserted himself into the conversation with Oli following quietly behind him. "Those barrels we threw into the river were full of sulfur. The stench will mask our scent for a while," Nat'an explained. "How are you feeling?" he asked Jeb.

"I'll be alright," Jeb clipped, "can you do something about her?" He pointed his thumb over his shoulder at Nila.

Nat'an looked past Jeb and examined Nila from afar before making his way over to her.

Rosa let out a soft, defensive growl at the chief as he approached.

"Rosa!" Jeb barked.

The mastiff stopped, let out a small whimper, and laid her head on the ground.

Nat'an knelt down in front of Nila and gave Rosa a soft pat on her head. "How was she before you got to us?" He asked as he pressed his fingers behind Nila's jaw.

"She looked a lot better than phat," Jeb answered.

Nat'an continued physically assessing her. "Olsdeyr," he called over his shoulder.

Oli snapped to attention.

"Go find Pik and Manson. Tell them to grab my medicine pack and meet me at the river."

"Got it," Oli nodded. He turned and went off into the camp.

Nat'an scooped Nila off the mastiff and carried her away. Rosa jumped to her feet and followed the chief closely.

"Rosa," Jeb called the mastiff. She whimpered and went back to him. He petted her wrinkled, brown forehead with a smirk, "she'll be alright. Good girl."

Theo stood to help Jeb climb Rosa's back and the three of them followed after Nat'an. Rhan fed Mak'tae a piece of dried meat, scratched him beneath his beak, and went off to join the group.

They walked through the patches of dry brush and back to the river. It was calm under the moonlight. Besides an occasional buzz of the jumping bugs in the grass, the night was silent. No screams or voices to be heard, there wasn't a wagon followed by armored knights or guards stamping along the cobbled roads. Even the camp was too far from the bank to break the veil of serenity.

Nat'an stepped down into the water. It rippled and distorted the reflected moon where he carefully held Nila's body afloat. Her pale, corpse-like face in the soft moonlight nearly broke Theo.

His heart sank into his stomach, his eyes started to burn, and the knot in his throat made it difficult to hold everything back. Different emotions swirled in between his head and heart.

Over the last week, the prince had said goodbye to his mother, watched Ashti lose her life to save him, saw an innocent guard die to protect him, an entire tribe was brutally attacked in pursuit of him, and now Nila was laying lifeless in the river because she held off the attackers so he could escape.

How did this happen? Theo thought to himself remorsefully.

In his head, he replayed the events of the past week over and over again. For the first time since it happened, he felt the split on the bridge of his nose from when his father struck him across the face with his rings. The muscles around his ribs went tight as he felt the stab wound that began the first of many chaotic nights. He could feel the bumps of scar tissue underneath his torn, stained, and dirty shirt he'd woken up from his coma in.

He looked to Rhan who stood stoically like her father. She kept her shoulders back and her chin high. She hid it well but something in her eyes screamed pain.

Theo turned and looked down at Jeb who was seated on a small rock next to the riverbank. He was fiddling with his rolled pack before pulling out the pipe and a black drawstring pouch. He pinched some dried, reddish-brown pipeweed from the pouch and jammed it into the wooden bowl of the pipe with his thumb. He did this two more times before smacking the pipe against the heel of his palm and setting the mouthpiece between his teeth.

Jeb snapped his fingers and a small flame burned from the tip of his thumb. He turned it against the dried plant, took a couple of puffs, and the bowl burned a low red. He filled his cheeks and let the first bit of smoke roll from his lips. After a second hit, Jeb began puffing out smoke rings that floated up in the air and danced on the breeze.

Footsteps in the brush broke the silent night and stole Theo's attention.

It was Oli and two others. Theo recognized the first man, it was the same horned man who helped them onto the pontoon that morning. The other was a tall, dark woman with a staff. Her hair was braided in thick tails that rested on her chest like Rhan's. Her ears were large and fawn-like, holding back the braids from her face. The tip of her nose was wide and leathery black. White spots dotted the bridge between her eyes and stopped below her brow.

Oli stepped out of the way and the other two stepped into the river with Nat'an.

The horned man Theo initially recognized held a rucksack open over the water for Nat'an while the woman stood and looked down at Nila's face.

The woman carefully placed the tip of her middle finger against Nila's forehead. "She's still in there—" the woman said, "barely, but she's here."

"Can we bring her out?" Nat'an asked as he reached into the open rucksack.

"We have to move quickly," the woman nodded. She took her twisted, wooden staff in both hands and hovered it over Nila's chest. The top end of the staff started to unravel and like a blossoming flower, it unrolled three green leaves around a soft amber light shining from the center of the now opened staff. Little orbs of light floated into the sky and a couple of them interrupted Jeb's perfect rings.

"Let us get started then," Nat'an sighed. He pulled his hand from under Nila out of the water. Her body bobbed on the surface before floating on her own.

The woman reached into a pocket of her tunic and pulled out a small purple crystal with veins of white inside it. She carefully handed the gem to the horned man. He raised the gem to the soft amber light coming from the green leaves of the staff's head and after a couple of seconds, the rock floated among the lights.

Nat'an reached into the rucksack and pulled out an empty vial with a couple of greenish-brown leaves. He took his other hand and reached into the bag again, coming out with a small mortar and pestle.

He dropped the leaves into the stone bowl and began crushing them. The dried, crispy ends pulverized into dust that mixed with the mush of the more preserved parts of the leaves. After a couple of seconds of pulverizing he had a white paste in the bowl.

He took the vial and uncorked its top between his teeth. Being careful not to lose any, Nat'an scraped the paste into the container. Once all of the leaf goo was collected, he dunked the entire bottle into the river.

"Pik, go ahead and begin," Nat'an said to the woman with the staff around the cork in his mouth.

She nodded and started moving her staff in a circle over Nila's chest. The soft amber orbs stopped floating up into the night sky with Jeb's smoke rings and settled against Nila's body.

Pik continued moving the staff in the air until the orbs of light began to bead like sweat off Nila's pale, ghostly skin. The amber hue of the orbs was replaced by a swirling black and gray smoke.

"Montiak, sa'frae bonotio," Pik recited under her breath.

The beads of black and gray slowly lifted off the unconscious elf's body, filling the space between the staff's gem and Nila's chest.

Nat'an took the vial out of the water, pressed his thumb against the opening, and shook vigorously over his shoulder. The white paste was now a green-ish-blue sludge that coated the inside of the vial.

He took his thumb off the mouth of the container and held it in the open space between the floating beads of black that came from Nila's body.

Pik stopped her staff and started circling the other direction with it.

One by one, the black beads were sucked into the vial, turning the green-ish-blue sludge clear like water.

Nat'an took the cork from his mouth and tightly secured it on the vial. He washed the residual paste on the mouth of the bottle in the river and then handed it to the horned man with the rucksack.

The chief knelt down, his chest still above the water, and held his arms out under Nila.

Pik stopped circling her staff and turned the still floating gem towards the sky. The leaves slowly curled their way back into the head of the staff and the amber light faded. She reached up and pulled the purple crystal out of the air and pocketed it.

Nila lost her buoyancy and splashed into the river. Nat'an caught her, pulling her from under the water, and he stood with her in his arms.

The color quickly returned to Nila's face and her pointed ears twitched with life. Her eyes blinked open and she squinted to adjust to the moonlight. "Oh...hello," Nila smiled weakly at Nat'an. She rolled her head back and stuck her tongue out pretending to be dead.

Nat'an chuckled and carried her out of the water.

"No?" Nila sighed playfully, her tongue still out and eyes closed. "I'm not breathing, you're going to have to—give me—" she pulled her head up, opened her eyes, and looked at Jeb. "What's it called when he kisses air into me?"

Jeb raised an eyebrow and puffed out another smoke ring, "mouth to mouth."

Nila nodded with a wink and ragdolled in Nat'an's arms again.

The chief shook his head with a smile as he carefully set her against the rock beneath Jeb.

Her eyes burst open and she tried to sit up.

"Whoa, easy there," Nat'an dropped to her side and caught her as she fell forward. "Your body is going to take some time to adjust and heal. The paralysis should subside soon."

He held a hand over his shoulder and the horned man placed the clear vial in his palm.

"Take this in the morning after you eat," Nat'an instructed, handing her the container. "It's going to weaken you a little so wait until it's safe to sit for a while."

Nila rolled back against the rock smiling at Nat'an, "I still think I could use mouth to mouth."

Nat'an smiled again and shook his head. He leaned in and as a friendly gesture, pressed his lips against her cheek. "I'm flattered," he said as he pulled back and saw her playful frown, "maybe another time."

BURNING EAGLE

The horned man ran off ahead towards camp while Nila dramatically insisted on being carried by Nat'an until her legs regained their strength. Rhan and Oli paced behind the chief with Pik between them, leaving Theo and Jeb behind at the riverbank.

Theo turned to follow the rest but stopped when he noticed Jeb was still puffing his pipe on the rock. "Are you coming?" The prince asked, retracing his steps. "Something on your mind?"

Jeb took a long pull from his pipe and let the smoke roll over his lips into his nose. "Just—remembering something—it's nothing."

He took the pipe, turned it upside down, and tapped the side of the bowl against the rock under him. With his other hand, he twitched his fingers as if he were playing the piano, and with the chime of three notes out of thin air, an ethereal hand formed under him. The hand lifted Jeb into the air, carrying him up the trail.

"How do you do that?" Theo asked excitedly.

"It's a talent," Jeb chuckled over his shoulder. "My mother taught it to me."

Theo chased after the floating hand, "can you teach me?"

"Depends..." Jeb shrugged, sinking back into the palm of the purple hand and resting his head against the fingers, "can you play?"

The familiar strum of metal strings filled the air before Theo could answer. It wasn't the smooth, acoustic of his guitar, there was a higher twang to the chords. Theo looked at Jeb and saw a banjo resting against his chest.

"Where—"

"Like I said, kid," Jeb smirked and closed his eyes, "it's a talent."

"How do I learn?" Theo begged.

Jeb turned his head upwards and raised a curious eyebrow. Theo could see him processing his thoughts with his face.

"What do you *want* to learn?" Jeb asked.

Theo pondered for a second, "will you teach me the guitar?"

A proud but surprised grin curled between Jeb's white mutton chops. "I could do that," he said, "let's talk about it in the morning." He relaxed into the purple hand again and let out a soft whistle to accompany his banjo.

Theo relished the entertainment as they both made their way back to camp.

Everyone was sitting outside their tents around the central fire. Fish and vegetables stabbed on stakes in the ground dangled over the flames and cooked in the smoke. In the middle of the burning wood and coals that fueled the fire was a large steaming clay pot.

A tall, dark, slender man with a mound of locks pulled back behind his head handed Theo a bowl and a piece of bread.

"Have you ever eaten camp-style?" Jeb asked as the hand gently set him on the ground before vanishing. He reached up, taking a bowl and some bread from the tall man, "there are some rules but nothing you're going to get in trouble over. Stick to my side kid and make sure you get enough."

Theo happily tailed Jeb as he ladled the chunky, brown stew from the clay pot into his bowl. He pinched a decent handful of fish off the stake and plopped it into his soup.

"Now these babies," Jeb smirked as he pulled a charred, rainbow-colored cob of corn from the fire. "This is one of many contributions the Okota tribe has given to society. Forget gold and all the treasures in the world. This—" he waved the corn in the air, "this is what real happiness tastes like."

Theo chuckled at Jeb's excitement and took his own cob.

Jeb led Theo through the camp and found a nice open spot near Rhan, Oli, Nila, and Nat'an.

Everyone talked and ate happily around the fire. A much-needed break from the chaos of the past week. Soft flute, tapping drums, and the rumble of a reeded instrument that Theo had never heard before filled the quiet night air around the camp.

The prince looked around, embracing the revelry with joy. He filled his empty stomach, going back for seconds after Jeb told him it was acceptable, and he savored every tasty bite.

Once the food was gone and some went around collecting bowls, the camp chatter started to die down.

"Your Highness," Nat'an called over to Theo.

The prince turned to the chief who was offering him a cup.

"Something to restore your energy," Nat'an said.

Theo accepted and took a sip. A sweet juice coated his tongue before settling into his stomach. Tingles shot up his spine causing his muscles to flex. It felt like the potion Alice had given him. All the worries, anxieties, and fears washed from his body as his muscles relaxed. He took another sip and quietly listened to the music.

A few minutes passed, the instruments started to fade, and

Nat'an rose from his seat. "My friends," he addressed the entire camp, "we give thanks to the creator for giving us this meal. Providing us with rivers full of fish, the trees she provides us to stay warm, and the berries we drink to restore our health. Thank you for these gifts."

Everyone bowed their heads and closed their eyes.

Theo watched for a moment and then followed suit, cautiously peeking from the corner of his eyes.

"We are hurting tonight. Our kin—" he looked to his left at Rhan, "our brothers and sisters of the plains have been wounded by an attack last night. Many have been scattered to the wilds in hopes of finding refuge. Some were not able to escape."

There was a sharp feeling in the air around the camp as the fire flickered.

"I pray that the ancestors are watching over those who might have been captured. But more importantly, I hope those who have gone to join the ancestors can find their way from this world." Nat'an paused, the crackle of the fire sending sparks into the dark sky. "As a tribe, we mourn those who can no longer be by our side." He reached down, placing a hand on Rhan's shoulder. "May their mortal forms return to the earth mother and their souls journey to the heavens beyond." He drew a shaky, deep breath. Theo could see his hands were trembling but he hid it well on his face. "In our grief, we are also given a blessing."

The chief released Rhan's shoulder and turned into his tent. He poked his head through the canvas door and came back out with a familiar headdress of feathers. Blotches of dried blood still stained the vibrant colored beads.

"It is uncustomary for the rite of the chieftain to be delivered between tribes," Nat'an explained soberly, "but what good is a tradition that cannot adapt to the ever-changing world we live in?" He stared at the feathers in his hands, examining the stains with pain in his eyes. "We grieve the loss of one of the greatest chiefs any of our tribes could have asked for. My uncle preserved our people's traditions while embracing new ones. I don't think there would be a better way to honor his legacy and the monumental successor who's rare gift from the creator will heal her people." He stepped behind Rhan and held the Woyan feather bonnet over her head. "Today we witnessed the dawn of a new chief as she flew into battle on the back of a flaming eagle. Risking her own life to save not just one, but all of our lives."

Two more beings stepped up next to Nat'an. One held a cup and the other had a wooden staff in their hand. They were decorated with beads, leather, and feathers.

"Through this feat, she has completed her trials of becoming chief," Nat'an continued.

The being with the cup knelt down in front of Rhan and held it to her lips.

Rhan nodded and drank from the cup.

"Rhan'takono-mua'vo, as chieftain of the mother tribe and a medicine healer, you take the duties of your ancestors and swear a life of leadership to your people. To protect them—"

The being with the staff tapped once against the ground and the sound of rattling came from inside the stick.

"To heal them—"

Again the staff clicked against the ground and rattled.

"And to teach them—"

The staff rattled once more.

"Under the watch of the ancestors and with the gifts of the creator herself," Nat'an lowered the headdress on Rhan's head, "I pass the mantle of Chief Ta'goda-mua'vo, the Raging Bear, to his only daughter."

Rhan closed her eyes and took a deep breath.

Nat'an rested the bonnet on top of Rhan's head ceremoniously. He pulled a brown and white owlbear feather from his belt and carefully added it to the front of the blood-stained collection.

"Rise, Chief Rhan'takono-mua'vo, Burning Eagle of the Woya."

The drums began booming to a heavy beat.

Rhan slowly rose to her feet, her eyes locked on the fire in front of her.

The being with the staff lifted the rattling stick over their head and shook it to the beat.

Chief Nat'an threw his head back and sang into the sky. His voice carried like a wolf howling to the moon.

Music filled the camp again and everyone joined in.

Theo felt it swell in his chest. The drumming and the singing. Then, just when he thought it was over, Chief Rhan started stamping in the dirt around the fire.

She danced around the flames as Nat'an continued to sing over the tribe. Sweat beaded on her forehead, trickling out from beneath the headdress, and flinging off her face as she spun.

Theo watched in amazement at every action, movement, and step. He felt the swirl of energy around him and he let it take him away.

The fire started to flare with flashes of green, blue, and purple. Rhan jumped, twirled, dropped, and danced until she could no longer stand. She collapsed into Nat'an's arms and the camp went silent.

"When you awake," Nat'an said softly to the now fading Rhan, "your journey will begin. May the ancestors guide you in the plains of dreams."

Rhan closed her eyes with a smile.

The tribe remained silent until Nat'an carried his cousin into his tent and then returned without her. The two beings carrying the staff and cup followed him in but never came out.

Slowly, the rest of the evening went on. Many of the tribe's people went down for the night, disappearing into their own tents, and eventually, the fire died down with Theo alone outside.

The prince sat outside of Nat'an's tent, staring up into the sky with his knees hugged to his chest. Chirps echoed over the soft trickling sounds of the distant river. He was restless and his anxious mind wouldn't slow down. He tried to distract himself but the dark void of the night sky offered him no solace. The moon's light masked most of the constellations but there was one star that twinkled like shining silver. At first, he thought it was a shooting star about to streak across the sky but it never moved. The silver star hung on the curtain of night. It made him feel safe.

"How did this happen?" he asked the star.

There was no answer. He didn't expect one. It was comforting to get off his chest.

A soft breeze brushed his face like two hands cupping his cheeks. Something his mother used to do.

"I wish we could talk *now*," Theo sighed, "it's been a week. The craziest week I've ever lived." He unfolded himself and laid back in the patchy grass. Something painfully pressed against his side. It was the pommel of his mother's saber still secured to his hip.

He grabbed the pearl hilt and pulled the saber from its sheath. The blade glistened in the moonlight as he held it up in front of his face.

Theo examined the handle, thinking about what his mother carried it for. He'd never seen her fight with it but she carried it wherever she could. It was never anything more than a ceremonial decoration she would use during the knighting event.

Theo looked at the tip of the blade that was tarnished with dark, dried blood.

It made him think about all that training the king forced him into. Learning to fight and kill his opponents at all costs. He was only a kid. He and Oli both.

"Was he always a monster?" Theo asked the star.

The air around him went still for a moment.

"Did you know—" a woman's voice filled the air, causing Theo to jump, "I personally knew your mother." A sleepy-eyed Rhan stepped out of Nat'an's tent. She carried two cups and offered one to Theo.

He sat up with the saber in his lap and took the cup. "How much did you—"

"Just the last part," Rhan shrugged, "I don't know how long you've been talking to her. But I don't—I don't blame you."

Theo heard the knot in her throat. "How are you feeling?" He tried to change the subject.

"Still a bit numb," Rhan shrugged. She sat down next to him and sipped from the drink. "Trying to process everything at once has been difficult and it's drained me." Rhan looked off into the sky, "Your mother—" she hesitated, "she was—I wish—"

"It's okay," Theo said, taking a sip from his cup. The familiar sweet flavor coated his throat and tongue again, calming the few emotions he had left.

"It's just—" Rhan tried to get out, "she did so much for my tribe and our people. When we received word she'd passed—" her words caught in the back of her throat.

"How did you know her?" Theo asked.

"She saved us," Rhan answered, "when I was a little girl our tribe suffered from a drought. A fire erupted outside our camp one night and it destroyed our crops. We had to release our animals into the wild and after that night, we had nothing. My father fought tirelessly against the fires but nothing could be saved. By morning, we were left to the elements."

Theo turned and watched her. He could see the building pain in her eyes.

"But your mother," Rhan continued, "she personally escorted a caravan of supplies. Food, water, seeds, livestock. She saved my tribe from extinction."

"I never knew that," Theo frowned, "she was always away on what I was told were diplomacy vacations."

"That's what she did with my people," Rhan broke a smile.

"It wasn't what the king wanted her doing," Theo sighed, "he told me that she was building bad relations. Keeping the needy people coming to our home. Exposing our people to—to these—"

"Savages?" Rhan cut in.

Theo gave her a guilty nod.

"Do you still think we're—"

"The last thing to ever come across my mind," Theo promised. "I knew that my life was always different from others. I was born a prince and trained from early on to think a certain way. I didn't know there were even other people out there. Two weeks ago, you could have told me that elves were real and I would have scoffed at you."

"Are you serious?" Rhan blinked in astonishment, "your best friend is an elf."

"I had no idea," Theo shrugged.

"And orcs like me?"

Theo shook his head, "Fairy tales."

"Your mother never told you about us?" Rhan deflated.

Theo shook his head again. "I thought she was always telling me stories or something. The king always degraded them to nothing more than children's tales of fantasy."

Rhan swallowed hard. She opened her mouth to speak but then pursed her lips, stopping herself.

"What?" Theo looked at her.

"You're heading into something—this whole escape you've been on for the last week—it's going to tear you apart," she warned. "You will be tested and held accountable for things you never did. Things you probably have no idea even happened."

Theo furrowed his brow.

"Your family has left a scar on this world. Not just your father, but his father, and grandfather," Rhan sighed. "They did horrible things and have terrified the world," she shifted uncomfortably. "*but—*" she hummed, trying to lift the conversation, "your mother also did a lot of good to the world. There are people out there who sing her praises and tell stories to their children about her."

Theo sipped his drink quietly. He didn't know what to say.

"I'm sorry," Rhan sighed, "I'm dumping this on you, and I shouldn't be."

"No, it's fine—"

"It's not though," Rhan shook her head, "I'm projecting my fears onto you."

"What do you fear? I watched you fall from the back of an eagle, dive into a canyon river, and take an evil sorcerer with you."

"That stuff is easy," Rhan said sheepishly, "you and I share a similar fate and that's what frightens me."

"What do you mean?"

Rhan took a deep breath, "We were born with a duty. You're a prince and I am the daughter of the chief. From the moment we could talk, people held high expectations for us."

Theo nodded in understanding.

"I always thought I would be able to take the mantle from my father when he was old. When he had nothing left to teach me and I knew what I was going to do." Tears began welling in her eyes, "now he's gone... without even a goodbye."

Theo stiffened as Rhan tried to choke back her pain.

"I'm the chief now—" she mumbled in personal reassurance, "just like that. There wasn't any warning, I had no idea it was going to happen. What am I supposed to do? Is there anything left of my tribe? Where are my people?" The floodgates burst open and Rhan began to sob.

Theo sat there uncomfortably for a moment before reaching over and carefully placing his hand on her shoulder. "Hey," he spoke calmly, "listen to me..."

Rhan wiped some of the tears from her cheeks.

"I wish I could tell you I understand what you're going through right now. One day I probably will. But I know where you're coming from and I get it. This overwhelming burden was placed on us before we even knew our own names. It consumes me at night thinking about what I have to live up to. A week ago that idea was just another fleeting thought. Now, I don't even know who I am." Theo paused. "I have no clue what being a leader is like. But I'm learning it. Watching your father and how he talked to his people. How to face grief and guilt with humility. I watched you take the most chaotic two days ever and persevere as if it was nothing."

Rhan broke a small smile.

"We've known each other for—a couple of days?" Theo continued, "never in my life would I have thought I could learn from a Woyan chief—" he stopped himself from rambling, "what I'm getting at is that you're going to make it through this. It's going to take some learning and a hell of a lot of work. But —*when*—we make it through this—whatever this is, I know without a shadow of a doubt that you will be the next great chief of your people."

CAMPFIRE COFFEE

Theo and Rhan talked for hours, each of them doing their share of releasing the pent-up emotions from the previous few days. They both cried, complained, and consoled each other. Theo told Rhan stories of things the king did that at the time didn't seem wrong, but now he understood the events that stained his memory.

Rhan returned it with stories of her father's teaching side and how angry he would get with her training. "Or there was the time—" she sniffed as she wiped tears from her cheeks, "he let me raise a chicken. I got attached to it, gave it a name, and even made it a necklace. Then one day he brought me a cleaver and told me it was time to kill the chicken."

Theo cupped his face in his hands, hiding his eyes, and shaking his head.

"We stood outside for hours as he went back and forth from yelling to whispering because I wouldn't do it," Rhan chuckled as she stared at the ground. "Eventually he took the cleaver from me and killed Pamb'o in front of me. I didn't talk to him for weeks."

"That's awful," Theo mumbled into his hands.

"I know!" Rhan agreed playfully. She rolled her head back and looked up at the early morning sky overhead. Purples and blues began turning into reds and oranges on the clouds.

Somebody crawled out of the opening of Nat'an's tent and Theo turned to see Oli staring back at him.

"Good morning," Oli greeted the two of them curiously.

"How'd you sleep?" Theo asked.

"I didn't," Oli grunted. He walked past them towards the fire pit from the night before and he started stoking the cold embers into a pile. With a few logs stacked on the mound of soot, he pulled two rocks from his pocket. Clacking the stones together he created sparks that became smoke under the wood. A few seconds later he had the fire relit.

"Hand me that kettle," Rhan asked Oli, pointing at the clay pot next to the fire pit, "I'll go get some water from the river."

Oli handed her the kettle and Rhan went off from the camp. The two boys sat silently in the cool morning air, neither of them wanting to break the silence first.

Oli focused on the fire, poking and prodding it every so often. Occasionally he would add another log.

Theo stared at the cup in his hand, sipping the last bit of his drink, and then pretending to keep drinking.

"How'd you sleep last night?" Oli finally spoke, still keeping his eyes on the fire.

"Oh—I, uhh—we didn't sleep," Theo stumbled over himself.

Oli glanced over his shoulder with another curious look.

"We talked all night," Theo pushed on, "she and I have pretty similar lives. At least—up to the point where *my* father is trying to kill me."

"Yeah," Oli said curtly, "it probably happens more often than you'd like to think."

Theo's hesitant pause told Oli that he didn't understand.

"You know, dads trying to kill their kids," Oli explained, "I'm sure you're not the only one running from a crazy parent."

"That's horrible," Theo frowned.

Oli shrugged, "Yeah, it is." He turned back and poked the fire some more.

"Oli," Theo said softly, "thank you. I'll never be able to say it enough. But from the most sincere, bottom of my heart—"

"There's nothing to thank me for," Oli cut him off as he tossed another fresh log into the blaze, "I'm just fulfilling my duty as one of the king's—" he caught himself.

"That's why I'm thanking you," Theo swallowed.

The silence lingered again.

"So what do you think we're going to do from here?" Oli asked, trying to change the subject.

"I have no idea," Theo sighed again, "I'm not even sure if this was a part of Alice's plan. We might be on our own here soon."

Oli shook his head, "there's no way your sister, as intelligent as she is, would have only had the escape part planned. There has to be a final rendezvous or something. A safe house or another contact who will take us to the next part."

"How do you know that?" Theo asked.

"It's logical," Oli shrugged, "she wouldn't have planned such a daring escape at the risk of her own life and the lives of others if she wasn't planning on doing something on the outside. There was more to this than just getting away from the king. She was on her own mission."

"That can't be—"

"Think about it," Oli turned back to the prince, "how could your sister have contact outside of the kingdom? She has spent her entire life within the walls."

"She's a well-known princess," Theo suggested, "people from

all over the world send her letters. You're suggesting someone within the castle set this up for her?"

"Exactly," Oli nodded, "I'm not sure who though—"

"It was my mother," Theo blurted out in revelation.

Oli locked eyes with the prince, "You don't think—"

"I don't want to," Theo stopped Oli from finishing his thought.

"Theo..." Oli swallowed hard.

"Is that fire ready?" Rhan's voice cut in. She came over the horizon, swinging the clay kettle in her hand. "I think—if Nat'an left his pack out—" she searched around the entrance to the chief's tent, "There you are!" She knelt down and plunged her hand into the rucksack from the night prior. She pulled out a pouch made of leather hide, "this will get a little kick into the morning."

She undid the drawstrings of the pouch and pulled out a small, thin, white piece of parchment. She turned the pouch over and a blackish-brown powder was dumped onto the parchment. With a small mound in the center, she closed the pouch and began twisting the parchment around the powder until it was in a tight ball. She took the lid off the kettle and dropped the parchment-wrapped powder into the water.

"What was that?" Oli furrowed his brow.

"It's something Nat'an brings from the port when he goes to trade with the city people," Rhan explained. "There are these beans that grow in faraway places and when you grind them down into a dust to steep it like tea, it makes an energizing drink that will carry you through the next few hours."

"Is it safe?" Theo asked.

"Safe? It hasn't killed anyone yet. We don't drink it all the time, only for special occasions like when tracking or hunting. It doesn't come to us often."

"What is it?" Oli grunted as Rhan placed the kettle into the fire.

"Nat'an says the people in the city call it *coffee*," Rhan answered.

"Is it good?" Theo asked.

Rhan laughed and then realized he was serious, "it tastes horrible."

"Then why drink it instead of tea?" Oli frowned.

"Just trust me," Rhan assured him. She carefully pulled the kettle off the fire and poured the brownish-black liquid into cups.

Theo took the drink and gave it a sniff. "I like the smell," he smiled.

"It's a great smell," Rhan nodded as she handed Oli a cup, "go easy, this stuff runs through you—"

"What in high hell is this?" Oli burst out as he spit out the first sip, "that's awful!"

"Take another sip," a new voice joined the circle.

The three of them turned as Nat'an stepped out of his tent in only his pants. Without another word, he moved around the two boys and bent down to grab a cup from the other side of the fire. "When I introduce you to my friend later, he'll tell you all about coffee and where to find it," he said, holding his cup towards Rhan.

Theo gave him a curious look as Rhan poured the chief's coffee.

"This is the last phase of your sister's escape plan," Nat'an explained to Theo, "we have one more handoff to get you to and then if all goes according to plan, you and Oli will be on the ocean headed far away from your father or his cronies."

"The ocean?" Oli burst out, nearly spilling his coffee.

"What is wrong with the ocean?" Nat'an frowned, looking at

Rhan with a confused look. She shrugged and set the kettle back on the fire.

"An untamable abyss of water filled with creatures and monsters while floating on a pontoon?" Oli blinked hysterically, "I'd rather turn around and take my chances for treason against the king!"

Nat'an cracked a small smile and shook his head, "my friend, the one I am taking you to meet, he likes to travel comfortably from time to time. You might not even notice you are sailing."

Oli turned to Theo and the two boys exchanged confused looks.

"Have faith," Nat'an chuckled before sipping his coffee, "you will be able to see his ships long before we reach the shore."

"*Ships*?" Theo repeated.

Nat'an nodded, "I doubt it will be a full armada, but he will have quite a fleet with him. Your sister is—or I should say *you are*—a high value asset that needs to be protected until you are out of the king's borders."

"Where are *we* going with this friend of *yours*?" Oli stiffened.

Nat'an's posture changed as he shifted on his feet, "he comes from another continent." The chief took a deep breath and another sip of his coffee, "he is a Grand Admiral where he comes from. That is why he has all these ships at his disposal." Nat'an looked at Theo and the prince could see the hesitance in his eyes.

"What?" Theo frowned.

Nat'an opened his mouth to speak but quickly shook his head, "nothing—not the time." He rolled his shoulders back and downed the end of his coffee. "If you are going to get to my friend in time, we should get moving. We have got a long trek ahead of us. If we have camp torn down in an hour, we might make it to the horses before mid-afternoon. That would get us to the coast by sunset and there is nothing more beautiful than watching the sun paint the clouds over the ocean." Nat'an turned on his heels, not waiting for a response, and began yelling over the camp. "Good morning my friends!" He shouted as he walked between the tents and pulled the canvas doors open.

Slowly, the tents were vacated and the tribe sluggishly made their way to the fire.

A handful of them poured their own cups of coffee while others went down to the river to bathe and collect drinking water.

A stout, broad shouldered man with a black beard trimmed close to his face pulled out some of the leftover food from the evening before and dished it out.

After a little bit of refueling, the groggy cloud over the camp turned into a lively atmosphere. Everyone chatted or sang as they began disassembling the tents and packed everything down. Just shy of an hour later, the entire camp was gone and the fire was smothered.

"Alright," Nat'an clapped his hands as he hoisted his rucksack over his shoulder. He pushed his way past the tribe and jumped up on a rock so he was looking over the group, "we have a lot of ground to cover before dark. Stick together, watch your surroundings, and stay alert!" he warned. "We were lucky to rest through the night but we are still being pursued. Any sign of the lycanfolk or the man in the mask means danger." He turned and looked at five members of the tribe who were dressed in darker colors and had bands of black, red, and yellow painted across their faces. "Get going and make sure the path is clear ahead. We will meet you at the first checkpoint. Stay hidden and out of sight. We do not need to be seen by wanderers or roving patrols if the king has already mobilized this far."

All five of them nodded and took off running.

Nat'an jumped down from the rock and began walking in the same direction, "let us get moving!"

Together, everyone started their trek behind the chief. Theo stuck close to Oli who was walking side by side with Rhan and talking. He couldn't hear any of it but he could tell Oli was in full protection mode.

"Hey kid," a voice stole the prince's attention. He turned to see Jeb walking next to him.

"Good morning," Theo greeted him with a smile, "how did you sleep last night?"

Jeb gave a small chuckle and stretched his back, "I can't say it was all that good but any sleep right now is better than nothing, right?"

"That's true," Theo nodded, "how's Nila feeling?"

Jeb craned his neck trying to look through the pack of people walking in front of them, "Hang on," he sighed. With a flourish of his wrist, the familiar ethereal hand formed under his feet and lifted him up just enough to see. "I'd say she's doing alright," he said, pointing towards the front of the pack.

Theo craned his neck to see past Oli's shoulder and there at the front alongside Nat'an was the dark mane of hair with long pointed ears poking out of the sides.

"She's a big fan of Nat'an, isn't she?" Theo chuckled.

"She's a fan of a lot of things," Jeb smirked as the hand lowered him to the ground and onto his feet again. "I think she's playing this cool, you should have seen her when we met an infernal woman who was the reigning fight-ring champ of her village. Nila was sure it was love at first sight and was ready to leave the mercenary life for her. Turned out the woman was wanted for murder and betrayal of a crime syndicate in the city."

Theo looked down at Jeb confused.

"What?" Jeb raised an eyebrow.

"What's an *infernal*?" the prince asked.

Jeb eyed Theo skeptically, trying to decide if he was joking. "Has there ever been anyone back home who didn't look like your family?" he frowned.

"Like—" Theo pointed at his ears.

"That's one of them," Jeb nodded patiently, "but beyond that, have you ever met anyone who was of a different race?"

Theo thought for a moment, "Oli was the only person I knew who had any significant traits but up until last week I never thought about it."

Jeb let out a small sigh, "this world your father's hidden from you is full of people of all sorts of descents." He pointed around the tribe, "elves, orcs, infernals, dragon-kin, goliaths, and giant-folk," he listed. "I come from a long line of halflings. My people are artisans and craftsmen with ancient traditions in the fine arts of fermentation, music, and tinkering."

Theo nodded along as he absorbed the information.

"Infernals are folks whose ancestry traces back to the demon conquests of another age. Do you remember the gentleman who manned the canoe that transferred us onto Nat'an's pontoon before we were attacked? His name is Manson, he's of infernal decent."

"The one with the—" Theo raised two fingers against his forehead.

"Yes," Jeb nodded, "but never do that again. There are folks who don't like infernals in certain places—kind of like your father—who use that as a derogatory gesture. It's got racist connotations."

Theo quickly shot his hand down to his side.

"It's okay," Jeb assured him, "you're learning about an entire world you didn't know existed. Just—try to refrain from making comments on others' appearances."

Theo nodded.

"But back to the lesson," Jeb smiled, "infernals do have

horns. Some even have tails and hooves. But it varies from bloodline to bloodline."

Theo tried to formulate a response but was left speechless.

"I know this is a lot of information on your mind," Jeb continued, "it sounds like I'm sticking to your side for a while so if you find something you have questions about, come grab me and we'll talk privately."

RIDING THE PLAINS

They hiked for hours through the tall grasses, over rock outcroppings, up and around hills, and through small rivers and creeks. Theo was growing delusional as his legs burned and he wasn't sure he could carry himself much further. But they continued on.

After a few hours, Oli slowed his pace with Rhan and fell back with the prince and Jeb. "Here, take some of this," Oli said, offering a small, tan pouch to Theo.

"What is it?" Theo asked.

"Rhan says they'll give you strength."

Theo gave Oli a curious look before taking a pinch of the black and white seeds in the pouch.

"By the sound of it, this is all we're gonna have for a while," Oli said

"Try 'em, kid," Jeb joined in, "it'll give you some sustenance and enough energy to get you to the checkpoint." He reached up and took a pinch from the pouch. Throwing his head back, Jeb dropped the clump of seeds into his mouth. "Just be careful—" he swallowed, "the little suckers get stuck in your teeth."

Theo drew in a deep breath and followed suit. He chewed

and swallowed the seeds and waited a couple of seconds but nothing happened.

"I don't feel any different," Theo frowned.

Jeb laughed, "why would you? It's just normal food. No different than your dried jerky or stale bread on the road. Let it digest and in a little bit, you'll be fueled for a while. Nothing more than a snack."

Theo's face grew hot and red from embarrassment. He'd grown so accustomed to everything they'd given him having some magnificent magic effect.

"Rhan said I could keep this bag so if you want some more, let me know," Oli offered. He closed the pouch and hung it on his belt next to his sword. "How're you holding up, Your High—Theo?" Oli corrected himself.

"I'm alright," Theo lied. He was exhausted. This was more hiking than he'd ever done in his life. "It's a bit hot for my liking but I think I will manage."

"Makes you wish you had gone with us on training hikes back home, huh?" Oli teased.

Theo stared back at Oli confused.

"What? You don't remember always leaving right before they made us go for a long hike around the castle walls?"

"No," Theo shook his head, "I didn't even know I was missing any training."

"What did you think happened after you would leave?"

"I just assumed it was a boarding school," Theo shrugged. "I genuinely thought that you all lived on the grounds. That's what the guard does."

"In shifts," Oli clipped.

"Yeah, I know that now," Theo said, "I just never gave it much more thought. I had other things to think about after I left training."

"Like what?" Oli raised a skeptical eyebrow.

"Well, usually after training I'd go study with my tutors. Foreign policy, military tactic training, family history classes. Did you know the king used to make me stand for hours a day beside his throne while he and his advisers discussed war efforts?"

"War efforts?" Oli furrowed his brow, "when were we at war?"

"Apparently all the time," Theo sighed. It felt like a weight off his shoulders he didn't know about. "It never crossed my mind how often they talked about moving the frontlines, attacking towns and adjacent villages. Now that I'm saying it out loud, I hear how horrifying it sounds."

"They never mentioned it in—" Oli froze, his eyes went wide with realization, "that's where they shipped everyone off to after I was injured, wasn't it?" He cupped his hands over his face, "They never mentioned where they took everyone. Just that they'd gone off to protect His Majesty's empire. I'm such an idiot!" Oli growled.

"We couldn't have known," Theo tried to console him, "we were kids. It was trained into us. Embedded into our heads. Everything we were taught as true—was nothing more than a ruse to make us—both of us—loyal to my father."

The word *father* tasted bitter in Theo's mouth. That monster who sat high atop a throne of death and dismay was the man who he called father. Theo's chest started to pound and it felt like his blood was going to boil inside of him.

"Theo?" Jeb interrupted.

The prince could feel his anger in his own face. He relaxed the muscles and felt the blood leave his cheeks, relieving the pressure he hadn't noticed was building. "Sorry—I just—that got me worked up," Theo mumbled.

"There's nothing to apologize for," Jeb assured him. "Both of you—" he gestured between the two boys, "are about to embark on a life-changing journey. It's going to tear you both to pieces along the way as you learn some of the harder-to-swallow truths about the world you live in. Much of which your family—" he looked sternly at Theo, "has been the root of."

Theo felt a tingle run down his spine.

"I advise you to keep your head down and try not to draw attention to yourselves," Jeb continued. He raised a hand up and snapped his fingers. Out of thin air, a crown appeared, dangling from Jeb's hand. Not just any crown, but Theo's crown. "But don't forget where you come from. You will be a leader of this world one day and hopefully will right some wrongs in an attempt to heal a world scarred by your ancestors."

Theo felt the weight on his shoulders return and it was overwhelming.

"Hey," Oli said with a soft punch in the prince's arm, "that's a long way from now. Don't let it scare you."

Theo swallowed hard. He understood why Oli had been keeping his distance over the past few days but to hear the sincerity in his voice eased the prince's anxieties.

"Whatever happens, I'll be at your side to keep you safe," Oli promised. "I trust your sister with my life and if she felt protected by this mission, I feel I can assure you that we will be okay." He held out the bag of seeds again.

Theo smiled and dropped another pinch into his mouth. He noticed his hunger was subsiding and his exhaustion was fading.

Another hour passed before the party reached the checkpoint. They crested a steep hill that overlooked a long, flat stretch of land. At the bottom of the other slope was a ring of wooden fences surrounding a herd of horses.

Nat'an waited for the entire tribe to safely make it down the hill before he followed. A handful of people undid the fences and dressed the horses for riding. They unfolded woven blankets from some of the camping gear and draped them over the steeds. By the time Nat'an rejoined the group, all the horses were ready to ride.

The chief pushed back to the front and talked to the lead rider. Theo watched and saw Manson, the infernal man from the river, atop the front horse. Manson had three streaks of red paint across both his cheeks. A bow and quiver were secured to his back along with a small, decorated shield bouncing against his hip.

Five more riders steered their horses around Nat'an as he spoke to Manson.

Theo tried to listen but they were too far for him to understand.

"Theo," Oli broke the prince's concentration. Theo glanced over at his companion who was offering to help him up onto Mak'tae's back. "Rhan has a horse and is going ahead with us and Nat'an."

Theo walked over and climbed up the owlbear.

"We're supposed to stick close to the chief and not stop until we hit the coast," Oli grunted as he pulled himself up.

As Theo situated himself behind Oli, he watched the five riders and Manson ride back up the hill they'd just come down.

"Where are they going?" Theo nudged Oli as he pulled Mak'tae's reins.

"Probably watching our backs before we start moving again."

"Do you think he's still following us?"

Oli glanced over his shoulder back at the prince, "if he survived that splashdown with Rhan, I would assume so. He's probably not happy either." He turned back and heeled Mak'-tae's sides.

The owlbear lurched forward and slowly sauntered behind the horses.

"We're going to ride fast," Nat'an addressed the party on

horseback, "stay alert and remember your groups. Manson and his riders are going to mask our trail in hopes of throwing off our stalker. If they're unsuccessful we'll begin breaking off. Each of you has your assigned duties to ensure everyone makes it home—"

Nat'an was interrupted by an incoming beast. It wasn't a wild animal but one of the scouts from earlier riding on a large, gray wolf.

The wolf-rider stopped on the other side of Nat'an who was now leaning off the side of his horse.

They kept their conversation to a whisper between each other and after a minute, the wolf-rider nodded and rode off from where he came.

Nat'an tugged his reins, spinning the horse around to face the party again, "Tight formations, listen for your group's command!" He yanked his reins, let out a yelp, and heeled his horse.

Altogether, the rest of the tribe let out their own cries into the sky before their mounts took off behind the chief.

"Hold on tight!" Oli warned Theo as he wrapped the reins around one of his hands. "Let's go, buddy!" He patted Mak'tae on the side of his neck.

The owlbear let out a small chirp and barreled after the galloping horses.

Theo wrapped himself tightly around Oli's torso trying not to fall off as Mak'tae bounded over rocks, through the tall grasses, and trudged across sandy patches of dirt. An hour passed before they stopped to let the animals rest at a small creek.

Rhan came over to pet Mak'tae while he lapped up as much water as his beak would hold.

"How're you guys holding up?" she asked Oli and Theo.

"You make it look easy," Oli grunted as he lowered himself

into the dirt to sit. "My legs burn from trying to stay up."

"Years of training," Rhan smirked. She pulled a small package from under her arm and tossed it to Oli.

"What's this?" He held the package up skeptically.

"It's your lunch."

Oli unfolded the package and inside were thin strips of dried, smoked, brown meat. The two boys exchanged a brief look at each other before each of them snatched a piece and started to gnaw on it.

Rhan moved over to them, crossing her ankles, and lowering herself onto the ground in front of Oli. She grabbed a piece from the unfolded pouch and proceeded to chew on one end "Nat'an thinks we're near the coast gate," she said while trying to grind the tough, leathery meat between her teeth. "If we keep the pace we're going and there aren't any distractions we should be there before sundown." She glanced over her shoulder at Mak'tae, "how's *he* holding up?"

"Hasn't missed a step," Oli grunted through the mouthful of meat.

She cracked a small smile, "He may be getting old, but Dad always said there was something special about him."

Rhan leaned over and pressed her head against the owlbear's forehead. Mak'tae turned his beak towards her with a disappointed look as she pulled her food away from him.

"I know," Rhan rolled her eyes playfully. She grabbed another piece of jerky from Oli and tossed it in the air towards Mak'tae. He snatched the meat in his beak and with both paws, he tore the food into smaller bites. Mak'tae gave a soft, happy hoot as he battled with the tough meat.

The three of them sat quietly, enjoying their all too brief snack and rest before horse hooves galloping in the distance filled the air, getting closer and louder.

Theo and Rhan jumped to their feet. Oli scrambled to grab

his sword from the ground and pushed in front of the prince and chief.

Four horses emerged from the cloud of dust that floated across the field. Theo instantly recognized Manson in the lead but something was wrong.

As the infernal got closer, Theo could see blood streaming down his face from the broken horn on his forehead. Manson's horse trotted past Theo, Rhan, and Oli, coming to a stop just short of Nat'an who was at the front of the pack.

Before the chief could say anything, Manson collapsed off the side of his saddle and into Nat'an's arms. He carefully lowered him to the ground, supporting Manson's head out of the dirt.

"We tried—" Manson grunted, "there were—uhg—it's an army—" he let out with his final breath. He grabbed Nat'an's shirt trying to hold on but his head slumped back into the chief's arms and his body went limp.

The ground began to rumble, causing Theo to stiffen as he turned and watched the marching army cresting over the hill on the horizon. Hundreds of armored soldiers in tight rows advanced towards them with banners standing tall among their ranks. Leading them was a familiar dark figure with two beings frantically sniffing the air.

"There's no way," Theo mumbled to himself.

"Move people!" Nat'an's voice erupted. He hoisted Manson's body over the back of his horse and climbed up to secure him. "Soma'ta, nothrir!" the chief commanded.

Before Theo could react, Oli grabbed him by the collar and yanked him towards Mak'tae.

An explosion rocked the earth as a massive ball of fire smashed into the dirt, almost knocking Theo off the owlbear as he climbed up.

"I'yato sotala!" Nat'an continued to shout over the chaos. He pulled the reins of his horse and the mount maneuvered itself to the back of the pack. "You three," he looked at Theo, Oli, and Rhan, "stick close to me and don't look back."

Another ball of fire fell from the sky, exploding overhead and raining down embers into the creek.

In groups, the party took off. The horses galloped and stamped across the fields.

Oli leaned down and petted the side of Mak'tae's neck. The owlbear let out a small, frightened chirp before charging after Nat'an and Rhan's horses.

Theo wrapped his arms tightly around Oli's midsection, trying not to fly off Mak'tae's back. He squeezed his legs tightly around the owlbear hoping it would help.

More and more explosions rocked the earth behind them. Narrowly missing the back of the party.

"Soma'ta, ito!" Nat'an cried out.

Two groups of riders broke off in opposite directions with their weapons drawn. In each group, one of the riders conjured orbs of energy that they would hurl towards the army still marching in the distance.

The orbs soared overhead and landed in the field between the two factions before absorbing into the earth.

Theo didn't understand the purpose of what was happening but he kept his head down and held tightly to Oli.

"Soma'ta, moyat!" Nat'an shouted again.

Another two groups broke from the pack, this time crossing each other's paths and then peeling off in different directions.

Nat'an called out three more times until the pack was only Theo, Oli, Rhan, three riders, and himself.

Theo could hear the erupting battle behind him and was too afraid to watch the onslaught. He felt the saber on his hip bouncing against his leg with every bound and leap Mak'tae made.

His surroundings blurred into streaks of green, brown, and blue as he locked his focus on the back of Rhan's head.

"Olsdeyr," Nat'an called to Oli, "the boulder to your right—head into it!"

"Into it?" Oli shouted back in confusion.

"Trust me!"

"You're not really going to—" Theo tried to ask but was cut short as Oli pulled the reins causing Mak'tae to jerk right.

Theo stared in fear as they charged towards the massive rock outcropping in the middle of the sandy patches of grass. He tried not to grip tighter onto Oli but his fear took over.

"Loosen—up—" Oli grunted.

Theo closed his eyes tightly and hid his face into Oli's back as Rhan drove her horse into the boulder. They were close behind her and he waited in horrified anticipation for the inevitable impact.

THE LOST KNIGHT

T he air around Theo changed. It was no longer the arid, dry feeling of the plains but humid, and the smell of salty seawater filled his nose.

"Am I—are we—dead?" Theo mumbled. He could still feel Oli's back and Mak'tae beneath him.

"No," Oli let out with a sigh, "we're here."

Theo hesitantly opened his eyes and picked his head up off of Oli's back. His vision took a moment to adjust but when the blurs became shapes, he stared in awe at the massive wooden hulls of the six ships drifting in the waters just off the coastline.

The sounds of crashing waves filled the air between barks and commands coming from the beach below. There were all sorts of beings moving in the sand. Some stayed near the rowboats that were tucked up on the beach while others toted crates and bags around.

It gave Theo a brief feeling of calm and serenity but that was quickly interrupted by the sound of horse hooves stamping up behind him.

Theo and Oli both swung around as Nat'an emerged from

inside a small tree trunk that looked like it was torn open from within.

As soon as the horse's tail flicked out of the tree, the trunk closed itself behind him and returned to normal again.

"What did we just—"

"Another time," Nat'an clipped as he steered past the boys. His horse trotted through the brush and down onto the beach.

"Stay close to me," Rhan said cautiously as she followed.

Theo glanced back at the empty space where they teleported through and there was no sign of any of it. No army, no rock, and no tear in the trunk. He was filled with questions but didn't know which one to ask first.

"Are those—" Oli whispered over his shoulder, gesturing towards the crowds on the beach, "pirates?"

Theo pulled himself over his friend to get a better look. It was hard at first to see them, but as they got closer he started to wonder the same thing.

Beings of all sizes and descents were dressed in all sorts of clothes. Some had on tattered military garb while others wore nothing but a pair of shredded pants that barely covered their legs. There were those with tattoos all over their bodies and others who looked like they were no older than the prince himself.

There were multiple groups of pirates taking on tasks all over the beach. Some lifted crates and other supplies onto small rowboats. Other groups team-lifted chests off the boats and carried them out of sight along the coast.

"Keep your head down," Oli said as he pulled Mak'tae's reins. The owlbear jolted forward and started sauntering through Rhan's tracks. "If these are really pirates, none of them can be trusted."

"If Nat'an trusts them, then I think we'll be okay," Theo shrugged, "I'm more worried about what's behind us."

"Just—be careful," Oli sighed.

They continued behind Rhan, both of them feeling curious eyes watching them as they got closer. Theo tried to duck behind Oli who was sitting up tall to help hide the prince. Oli turned his chin up to keep himself from staring at the eye-patched faces and tattoo-covered limbs.

Bouncing back and forth on the owlbear's back, Theo felt something bouncing on his hip. The weight of his crown tugged at his belt. He moved his hand to hide the exposed reminder of who he was, and something caught his hand.

He darted his eyes down, expecting to see one of the pirates grabbing him, but he saw the pearl hilt of his mother's saber. It was hanging in a weird way and for a moment Theo thought that the sword had purposely blocked him from his crown.

"No," he whispered to himself, shaking his head. He tried to grab the crown again and found his fingers entangled in the handguard of the saber. "Oli?"

"What—"

"ADMIRAL IS LANDING!" A heavy voice boomed over the beach.

Theo watched as everyone stopped what they were doing and rushed to the boats on the shore.

Floating along the soft waves was a slightly larger rowboat sailing up to the sandbanks. It landed on the beach and five beings climbed out. Two tall and slender elves, one with an eye patch, the other wearing a tricorn hat stood before a large, pale-gray man with tattoos and scars all over his bare torso. He towered from behind the elves, nearly masking them in his shadow. All three of them carried different swords on their belts. Two more beings stepped out of the other side as Theo and Oli came to a stop.

Nat'an moved his horse in front of the boys, blocking their view of the landing party. "Your Highness," the chief rumbled, something to his tone was stone cold and sharp, "this is where our journeys separate. My friend here is going to take you far from here where you will be safe. He will harbor you in his homeland per your sister's requests."

"But you're in danger too," Theo frowned, "you can't go home. They'll hunt you down for sure!"

"Try as they might, but it's my duty to make sure my people are safe."

Theo wanted to argue, the words sitting in his throat.

"I hope one day you understand the sacrifice a leader must make," Nat'an swallowed. "Maybe one day that lesson will help you heal the world." Without another word, the chief turned from Theo and climbed down from his horse on the opposite side.

The prince could hear him walk through the sand away from them and towards the water.

"You kids ready to set sail?" a familiar voice interrupted the moment.

Theo and Oli turned to see Nila and Jeb riding up next to them on Rosa.

"We will be," Oli clipped as he turned his attention back to the beach. He rolled his shoulders back and continued to scan the surroundings.

"I feel like—after all of this—I'm prepared for anything," Theo sighed playfully.

"Very funny," Nila chuckled, "in my two-hundred years of experience—"

"Two-hundred what?" Oli spun back around.

Nila smirked at him and gave him a wink.

Oli squinted at her skeptically.

"You boys are in for a whirlwind when you reach port," Jeb laughed. "I hope maybe our paths will cross again and we can share in some stories—"

"You're not coming with us?" Theo deflated.

Jeb's cheery expression diminished to a sobering frown. "Your sister only hired us to get you to Ta'goda. We have more than fulfilled our employment and our payment wasn't quite enough to charter—"

"You liar," Nila groaned as she smacked Jeb upside the back of his head. "You blew your cut in a tavern three days before our job. We could have had enough to charter something together but you had to buy drinks for those—those—what's the word?"

"Watch it," Jeb said defensively, "those folks were having a night out on the town. They were innocent farmers who came to meet people in the city. It's not my fault they decided to spend their evening with me at that bar."

"And they left with most of your money after you were too drunk to notice," Nila rolled her eyes.

"They what?" Jeb stiffened.

"I'm sure we could ask the Admiral—"

"Oh no, kid," Jeb threw his hands up, "we're—uh—how do I say this?"

"Don't ask me," Nila shook her head, "I'm still working on the language."

"We're not welcome in a lot of places," Jeb smiled guiltily.

Theo could feel Oli's back tense.

"But it's nothing," Nila tried to recover the conversation, "a few misunderstandings with previous employers. Many of them —" she glared down at the back of Jeb's head, "are angry spouse related."

"*His* angry spouse?" Rhan snorted.

"Never," Jeb sighed.

"You've lived quite the life," Theo laughed. "I hope we do see each other again. You still owe me a guitar lesson."

Jeb met Theo's eyes and gave him a devious smirk. "Do I now? Then what's that on your back?"

Theo spun around excitedly but there was nothing. Disappointed, he turned back to Jeb who was no longer there. Rosa was carrying them both quickly up the beach with a cloud of sand masking them as they vanished from sight.

"I'm gonna miss them," Rhan sighed.

"He was supposed to teach me to play—"

"Theo!" Nat'an's voice called from across the beach.

He spun back in the other direction and saw the chief standing next to one of the two beings he hadn't seen. They were tall and dark with a black hood masking their face.

"Theo!" Nat'an called again, this time gesturing for him to come down.

He carefully slid down Mak'tae's side but didn't move after a hand grabbed his shoulder.

"Your Highness..." Oli said softly so no one else could hear.

Theo looked up at his friend, their eyes meeting for only a second before the prince changed his motion to help Oli down off the owlbear.

"If anything happens to me," Oli whispered as he set his boots on the ground, "take the bear and run." Without another word, Oli walked towards Nat'an. As he took Theo's spot and approached the group, the final being came into view.

A dark, curly mound of hair much like Theo's rested beneath a tricorn hat. Their double-breasted coat and officer's uniform underneath was worn, soft, and a bit dirty.

There was a tingle in the back of Theo's head, deep behind his brain at the base of his skull. Something about this man was familiar. It was there in his mind but he couldn't put it together as the tingle became flashes of memories.

They had been to the castle before. Images of his mother laughing with this man. Screaming and sounds of glass crashing to the ground. The king's angry voice shouting unintelligible obscenities. Alice tucked into a dark closet holding Theo in fear.

"It's going to be okay," Alice whimpered in his ear.

Theo was thrown back into his body suddenly and he knew everything. He felt like a dark storm cloud had lifted from his mind and for the first time in a long time, he was free.

"James," Theo exhaled. The name fell from his mouth, dragging all the air from his lungs with it. Not thinking, his legs took off from beneath him. He sprinted past Oli and ignored the difficult loose sand. Charging at the group of sailors, the man in the worn officer's uniform stepped forward and threw his arms out.

"Theo!" he cried out as the prince slammed into his chest. The two embraced each other tightly and the sounds of muffled tears came from both of them.

"I—I forgot," Theo choked into the man's shoulder.

"You didn't," he assured the prince. "It's not your fault, none of this is."

"I forgot you," Theo continued to cry, "they made me forget you."

Floods of memories began to fill Theo's head. Holidays, festivals, ceremonies, and other tender family moments. James was there the entire time.

Each memory was interrupted by the blurring vision of a man in a black mask with long white hair forcing a drink into Theo's mouth.

"You're safe now," James said as he pulled back to look at Theo, "he can't hurt you now."

"This is real, right?" Theo swallowed nervously.

"Theodore," James looked into the prince's eyes, "I am your brother. You are the crowned prince and heir to our father's throne."

ABOUT THE AUTHOR

Geek by heart, author by trade.

Raised on a healthy diet of geek and pop culture, I have come to share my love and appreciation for role playing games, geek culture, and fantasy adventure. If it's random comic book fact, Star Wars trivia, or just the measly obscure movie reference, I'm there!

I hope you enjoyed
The Prince

Here is an excerpt from book two:
The Admiral

THE ADMIRAL
OLD FRIENDS

Jeb's back straightened and he swallowed nervously. "I—uh—"

Around the deck, the ship's crew scrambled to the lanterns and ignited the oil lamps, illuminating the night around the ship. Others climbed masts and ropes to find good spots where they could watch what was about to happen.

Jwala came lumbering up from the lower decks, rubbing his eyes and tying down his wild beard.

Ulrick crossed the deck toward the bow and reached across his torso drawing his curved scimitar from his belt.

"You really want to do this?" Jeb asked nervously.

"She's welcome to join you," Ulrick offered, pointing his blade at Nila.

"Oh no," Nila shook her head. "I'm not a part of this. If you kill him—" she nodded at Jeb, "you can add me to your crew or lock me in the brig. This is his fight."

"I'm so glad you agreed to this job with me," Jeb sighed sarcastically.

Jwala moved around the deck and stood next to Ulrick. He was still messing with his beard, braiding it and tying it until it was a stiff tail coming off his chin. Once he was satisfied, he undid his black vest, taking it off to reveal the chiseled and tattooed torso underneath. He rolled his shoulders back and raised his fists in front of his chest.

"Hold on—" Jeb burst out, "this is just you and me, yeah?"

"You know a Duel of Good Faith is for all of those you wronged," Ulrick reminded him.

"Okay, yeah," Jeb stalled, "but if that's how we're doing this, I've got to fight the entire ship."

"I fight for all of them," the helmsmen proclaimed with pride.

"Jwala, come on," Jeb said with his arms held out wide. "It wasn't that big of a deal between us, right?"

"You locked me in the brig of a sinking ship," Jwala answered dryly.

"Right," Jeb sighed in defeat. "Welp—" he clapped his hands together and took a fighting stance. He unclasped the torn cloak around his neck, letting it fall to the floor, and he began rolling his sleeves back. "The code states that all duels must be fought fairly."

Ulrick nodded in agreement.

"Two against one isn't fair," Jeb continued.

Ulrick's nostrils flared. "Anyone on this ship is fair game to choose," he offered. "But no one will stand by your side after everything you've done—"

"I choose the kid!" Jeb burst out, pointing his thumb over his shoulder.

Theo felt every muscle in his body tense and the hairs on his neck stood straight. "What— I can't—" Theo tried to protest.

"Come on, kid," Jeb begged. "I need a partner. You have to do this with me—"

"But Nila backed out," Theo reminded him.

"Yes," Jeb pursed his lips. "That's your choice as well, but I *need* this. I *need* you and that saber of yours."

Theo felt the weight of the blade dangling on his hip.

"He's not going to fight," Ulrick snarled. "That's out of bounds—"

"You said it yourself," Jeb turned back towards the captain, "anyone on the ship is fair game."

"He won't be a part of—"

"I'll do it," Theo announced over Ulrick.

The ship went silent. Only the steady creaking of the hull and the sloshing of the ocean hung over the deck.

Ulrick straightened for a moment and then returned to his fighting stance with his scimitar drawn in front with both hands. "Then so be it."

Theo took a deep, shaky breath as he slowly moved next to Jeb. He rolled his sleeves as high and tight as he could as his heartbeat steadily pounded in his chest. Taking his place in front of Jwala, Theo planted his feet and lowered himself into a defensive stance. He drew the silver blade that glinted in the lamplight.

"You sure about this, Theodore?" Jwala asked.

"No," Theo shook his head, "but everyone deserves a fighting chance." His hands started to sweat around the pearl handle and he could feel all of his weight in his knees. But something about this felt normal to the prince He had trained for so long for a moment like this. It was ingrained in him. He took another deep breath, rolling his shoulders back, and locked his focus on Ulrick's long, curved blade.

"Alright," Jeb cheered under his breath. "If you keep Ulrick from getting to me, I can take the dwarf."

Theo glanced over his shoulder at Jeb but the halfling began screaming and charging at Jwala. Jeb sprinted across the deck with his fist held high and he closed in on the helmsmen, leaping in the air just before coming down and striking him across the lower jaw.

Jwala took the hit but remained unphased. He gave a small chuckle before clasping his hands together and powerfully slamming them into Jeb's stomach.

The halfling was launched off his feet and sent backward across the deck. Right before he crashed to the wooden floor, an arcane purple hand snatched his collar and set him on his feet.

Jeb didn't hesitate and rushed Jwala again, his fist cocked as far back as he could manage.

Jwala braced, raising his arms together to block the blow, but when Jeb was within striking distance, he vanished.

Confused, Jwala dropped his guard to see what happened to the attack. As he pulled his arms apart, a voice chirped from behind him. "You're a lot tougher than I remember."

The dwarf spun around with a large swing but nothing was there.

With Jwala facing the other direction, Jeb reappeared in the same spot he had vanished from, arm high above his shoulder. "But still just as gullible," he laughed. The halfling aimed his punch at the back of Jwala's thick mane of dark dreadlocks.

"I don't think so," Ulrick growled. The captain leaped from his planted stance and body checked Jeb out of the air.

The halfling man went flying across the deck again, slamming into a loose pile of coiled ropes.

"We're not falling for your dirty tricks this time, Jerbalious," Ulrick barked. He stomped over toward where Jeb had landed with his scimitar ready to strike the ruined rope coils.

As the captain got closer, a flare shot out of the pile, high above the ship, and exploded overhead. Sparks of yellow, red, and orange rained down on the crew.

Ulrick wasn't amused. "Get out here and fight, you coward!" the captain snapped as he lunged at the ropes. His massive, muscular arms rippled as the blade cleaved through the thick ropes, sending frayed ends everywhere. But Jeb was gone again.

Theo stood frozen to his spot, his hands still trembling and sweating around the saber.

"Enough of the gimmicks!" Ulrick growled, scanning the deck.

"Fine," Jeb's voice echoed in the night air.

The entire crew jumped as they looked left and right searching for the halfling.

In the middle of the ship, Jeb rematerialized with his hands raised in surrender.

Ulrick and Jwala turned to face him and the captain pointed his scimitar at the halfling.

"Ya got me," Jeb sighed playfully. "Lock me up and throw away the key."

Ulrick looked over at Jwala and furrowed his brow, unsure about the situation. The captain gestured with his head at Jeb and Jwala nodded.

The helmsmen cautiously approached Jeb, his fists still raised and ready to fight.

Jeb smirked and pulled his hands down in front of him with his wrists together.

"You're not tryin' anything funny now, yeah?" Jwala grunted. He stopped just short of the halfling, waiting for a response.

"I can assure you," Jeb said calmly, "from the bottom of my heart and on the grave of my own mother... I am always trying something funny."

There was a burst of yellow light that shot from between Jeb's fingers and struck Jwala square in the chest. The sturdy dwarf went flying backward and smashed into Ulrick.

The two pirates landed in the messy pile of frayed ropes and tangled themselves together as they fought to get up.

Jeb turned to Theo with a mighty grin. "Sorry you had to get dragged into this, kid," he laughed, walking away from the chaos. "Negotiations are sometimes—messy." He crossed the deck and headed towards Theo. "You can put her away now," he gestured at the saber, "we're in charge—"

Jeb froze mid-step. He let out a confused chuckle before trying to walk forward. He wiggled and fought but neither of his legs would cooperate. "Just—a sec—" he grunted nervously.

"We're not finished!" Ulrick's voice boomed over the ship.

Vines of seaweed began to sprout from the wooden planks of the deck and wrapped themselves around Jeb's legs.

Theo shot his attention over to the pile of ropes as Ulrick and Jwala had escaped the mess and the captain was kneeling on the deck with had his hands pressed against the floor. The tattoos along his arms were glowing a deep, green color and shimmering energy flowed from his hands into the deck.

Jeb looked up at Theo and let out a defeated, lighthearted sigh. "It's always a surprise with these two."

"Coming from you?" Ulrick clipped.

Jeb's feet began to absorb into the deck with a similar deep-green arcane energy pulling him downward.

"Alright, kid," Jeb grinned nervously at Theo, "now would be a great time to step in and help." He swirled his hand and a translucent red ribbon shot across to Theo. It wrapped itself around the prince's wrists and started pulling him towards Ulrick.

Theo hesitated at first before his feet gave in to the dragging force of the ribbon. He moved across the deck and swung his saber at the ground. He could feel the ribbon pulling and tugging, trying to attack Ulrick's hands on the deck but he fought back.

The tip of the blade splintered the wood just inches from the captain's fingers and Ulrick ripped his hands back off the ground, breaking his enchantment.

Jeb sprang from the trap and kicked away the wilting seaweed. He flourished his hands together above his head and floating in the air over the halfling was a growing ball of purple and yellow light that swirled together. He pulled his hands apart and the colors split into separate whips in each hand. He flicked his wrist with the yellow arcane whip and bolts of electricity sparked as it cracked in the air in front of Jwala.

The red ribbon continued dragging Theo's arms and he swung the saber in the air in front of Ulrick, narrowly missing each hit as he tried to pull out of the magic binding.

Ulrick was quick, dodging each attack as Theo tried to refrain from landing any of them. His feet moved swiftly, countering each of Theo's movements. The prince shifted with the captain, placing his feet and leading as if the two were doing a dance.

Dangling from the masts above and perched on the side railing of the ship, members of the crew hooted, hollered, and cheered on the fight. Someone would call out wagers and sailors would throw small pouches of coin to each other.

Theo didn't notice any of it. His focus was tunneled in on Ulrick as the two continued spinning around each other.

"You're quick," the captain noted as he sucked in his stomach to avoid being slashed.

"I've—had some—training," Theo grunted between swings.

"It shows," Ulrick complimented. "Your brother taught you well. But—" he reached over his shoulder and out of thin air he pulled his scimitar from behind himself, "he's also my sparring partner."

Ulrick threw his blade in front of himself, catching Theo's saber mid-swing, and the two stood frozen in a stalemate. The prince could feel the overwhelming power in the goliath's bulking arms that kept him at bay.

"Your brother is a formidable adversary and dear friend," the goliath smirked. "I hope that doesn't change after this."

Before Theo could retort, Ulrick swept his legs out from beneath him and the prince hit the deck with a loud thud.

He blinked quickly to shake the distortion and dizziness. His vision cleared just in time to dodge Ulrick's next attack. The scimitar slammed into the deck, narrowly missing him as he rolled to the left. The prince jumped to his feet and held his saber at the ready.

Ulrick followed Theo, letting off a few small slashes that the prince parried to the side.

"I'm not sure—what to say," Theo panted between blocks. "Are you going to—"

"Kill you?" Ulrick chuckled with another light slash. "Far from it. I won't harm a single hair on your head. Admiral's orders."

"Then what are—we doing?"

"You're staying distracted," Ulrick smirked. The two froze as their blades clanged together. "I'm letting Jwala have some fun."

Theo furrowed his brow and looked over to the other side of the deck.

Jwala and Jeb were going back and forth as flashes of colors sparked and exploded between the two of them.

Ulrick took the opportunity and headbutted the prince square in the nose.

Everything began to spin for Theo. He was stunned and couldn't find his way out of it. He stumbled backward a few steps, almost falling to the floor. Something warm started to coat his upper lip and trail down his chin. He looked down and watched the drops of blood pooling at his feet. Theo shook his head and wiped his face with his forearm.

Ulrick stood ready for the next attack.

With his hands still bound by the ribbon, Theo charged the

captain. Their blades clashed as the prince swung viciously at the goliath. Ulrick had a slightly amused smirk as he returned the volley of attacks.

The two went back and forth for quite a while. Circling each other and changing the terrain as they climbed on or over things on the deck.

Overhead, the crowds of crew cheered even louder at the spectacle below.

Ulrick continued to play into each of the attacks and Theo was starting to pick up on it. The captain wasn't giving him a fighting chance, he was studying him. Carefully watching the prince's every move.

"You fight valiantly," Ulrick commended, "but you're out of practice. Going through the motions rather than executing."

"I can't tell you—how long it's been since—I've actually—done—this—"

"In time," Ulrick said.

"How about—right now?" Theo grunted.

The prince transitioned his stance, stepping forward into Ulrick. The Captain tried to counter with another step but Theo found his target.

With his saber, the prince moved Ulrick's weapon to the side and threw a sharp shoulder into the massive goliath's stomach. He hit the wall of muscle and felt all the air escape the captain's chest.

Letting out a pained wheeze, Ulrick stumbled over himself and landed on his back. He hit the deck with a booming thud and everything went silent.

Thank you for reading

The Prince

If you enjoyed this or any other adventures by Antony Soehner, consider leaving a review on Amazon, iTunes, or where ever you leave your book reviews. It's greatly appreciated and helps the author.

OTHER TITLES BY

ANTONY SOEHNER

<u>Gather the Party Trilogy</u>

Gather the Party

Unite the Party

Assemble the Party

<u>After School Adventure Series</u>

Beyond the Briar Patch

Into the Jungle

Lost in the Desert

<u>Dragon Siege Series</u>

Dragon Siege: Book 1

Dragon Siege: Book 2

Dragon Siege: Book 3

www.ingramcontent.com/pod-product-compliance
Lightning Source LLC
Chambersburg PA
CBHW020022310726
48970CB00007B/2161